ASK NOT

ASK NOT
Copyright © 2024 **Mary Schmidt.**

Script Marker
500 8th Avenue FRNT 3 #1560
Manhattan, NY, 10018
516-684-9243
www.Script-Marker.com

ISBN 979-8-89523-020-6 (Paperback)
ISBN 979-8-89523-021-3 (Ebook)

Printed in the United States of America.

ASK NOT

MARY M. SCHMIDT

Dedication

In Memory of Charles Butler
One Awesome Editor

Contents

1963

Katie Casey had her share of symptoms.

Ringing in her ears gave her headaches and insomnia.Her blood pressure was way too high. The pills Dr. Robinson had prescribed were not helping her, so she had stopped taking them. They kept her awake.

Tonight, however, she was having a beautiful dream. Perhaps that little nip of cooking sherry before bed had helped.

Katie saw herself in a posh hotel in New York. President Kennedy was there, ostensibly for a high-level meeting. The Secret Service had their encounter planned to perfection. On the lower level of this hotel there was the Grande Promenade: a corridor that seemed to extend forever, lined with phone booths. For a moment, Katie stirred, then went back to her dream.

There was a young girl, pouring coins into one of those phones, apparently weeping. Katie quickened her steps. She would not get involved in whatever oddity this was.

As she had been instructed by a Secret Service agent, Katie took the elevator to the top floor and followed the signs to the pool.

Again, the Secret Service, bless them, had left no stone unturned. They had taken care of her husband Ralph. Ralph was in the hotel garage, seated in the back of the presidential limousine, with its top down. An agent pretended to drive him down a packed boulevard. Four agents ran in place at the sides of the huge vehicle. Thousands of imaginary souls waved flags and cheered. A tape recorder played *Hail to the Chief.*

"Woo! Woo!" Ralph kept saying. This would keep him amused for the rest of his life.

Meanwhile, Katie was spirited up to the safe zone which had already been swept for any sort of listening device. There were none. No one need ever know.

The coast was clear. There was no Ralph. Neither was there the president's wife, Jackie. Those two would never find out.

"Ah, Mrs. Casey!" the president greeted her. He was dressed in his bathrobe and smoked a cigar.

"Mr. President!"

"Please, Darling. Jack."

Flustered, she stammered, "Hello, Jack! I'm Katie!"

"Katie," he moaned, savoring her name. They kissed deeply. He dropped his robe, under which he wore nothing at all, and assisted Katie out of her dress, and delicate underthings. Together they dived into the deep end of the pool and swam in laps like a pair of graceful koi in an aquarium.

They made slow and sweet love. Katie woke up with a gasp and a start. "Jack?" she called out, but not loudly enough to interrupt Ralph's snores.

Now she was fully awake. She sat up and got out of the bed. She was rather shocked that John F. Kennedy would ever consider doing such a thing. In reality, he was a head of state, married and the father of Caroline and John John plus one on the way. But in Katie's fantasy…

She got up from the bed where Ralph lay snoring and went downstairs. As was her custom she slept in the nude, and never even bothered to put on her robe when she left their bedroom. Ralph took a dim view of this.

"Suppose our son wants to raid the fridge at midnight and finds his mother on the sofa, stark raving naked?"

"Dickie never gets up at night."

"Suppose he does? He's seventeen. At that age, they get ideas."

"Dickie would sleep through a nuclear war."

"Not a good idea. Might be a Peeping Tom hanging around. He could look right in that front window and see you."

"On this street? If he looked at me, I doubt he'd be interested."

"Don't be too sure," Ralph muttered. "All kinds of perverts, out there. They got one last week in Silver Hill. It's getting awful."

Katie was way overweight. With her body unrestrained by bra or girdle, gobs of fat hung off her midsection like sacks of potatoes. Her nakedness was a challenge to those of lesser size. *If you don't like it, tough. I could not care less.*

In her living room, there were pictures of herself and Ralph at their wedding, and of their son Dickie as a little boy in a cowboy outfit. And, of course, an inaugural portrait of John F. Kennedy. Oh, she loved him. She wished she could be his mother, Rose. Or his glamourous wife, Jackie. One, the other, or a bizarre and Oedipal combination of both.

Here, on this sagging sofa, she had spent her happiest day a few years ago. Ralph had thought of taking his family to Washington for Kennedy's Inauguration. Then he backed out. "It might snow," was his reason. Never mind that he thought it would be too expensive.

It did snow, in large amounts.

"You can see more on the TV without freezing your big rear end off," Ralph reminded her.

"Ralph, please," Katie had said, "not in front of the children."

On a day so cold and clear the air sparkled, Kennedy took his oath as President of the United States. Katie was so blissful, she felt as if she had levitated from this sofa.

"And so, my fellow Americans, ask not what your country can do for you!"

"Happy now?" Ralph asked.

"This is the happiest day of my life!"

"Aw, come on!" said Ralph. He pointed to their elaborate wedding portrait. "I thought that was!" Katie could only weep for joy. How strange it was, to remember now how happy she had been then. It seemed so long ago.

The only other sign of life on the block was a light in Dan Doyle's study across the street. He was the only one here who did not work a nine-to-five schedule or have to commute. That's because he was the Dan Doyle, the bestselling novelist. What was he working on now? Perhaps it was what he called the ultimate sequel: *Moby Dick II: Raise the Pequod!*

Doyle's novel in progress had something to do with Moby Dick's look-alike grandson knocking over a luxury liner full of rich people. It was sure to be a blockbuster film.

For some obscure reason, Ralph did not approve of Dan Doyle. Ralph used to glare at Dan and ask Katie what his problem was.

"I don't believe he has one, Dear," she would say.

"What's with the beard? Is he trying to be some sort of beatnik?"

Katie just shook her head. Ralph was a great believer in conformity. Dan was the only one on this block with no resident family. To Ralph, this neighborhood was only for white married couples professing Christianity and raising children. They were only permitted to drive what his boy Dickie called boring sedans or even more boring station wagons. Doyle drove a Porsche. Once, on the highway, Doyle passed them going va-room! Ralph was clearly displeased.

Ralph is jealous. That was what Katie thought at first. Dan was too different for Ralph's limited tastes. She thought of a song about what Ralph preferred. *Little boxes, on a hillside, all made of ticky-tacky.*

Someone used to sing that. Katie jumped up with a start when she remembered who did: Michelle. Michelle, who used to strum her guitar and sing that song, so long ago.

No! No, don't let her into your mind!

Katie, a bit short of breath, sat back down on the sofa. Too disturbing! And yet, the portrait of John F. Kennedy took the place of Michelle's portrait when she could no longer stand the sight of it. That picture was up in the attic with the rest of Michelle's things. Up and forgotten, where Katie no longer had to deal with them.

Oh, but she did love John F. Kennedy! So much that anyone who did him harm would have to answer to her and would pay with his life. Simply watching him on TV brought her such joy.

Having him in the White House made her feel safe. She had not always been safe. As a child, she had been forced to learn that there are terrible things going on. John F. Kennedy was the knight who slew the dragon, of whom she was so afraid. As long as he remained in the White House, no more harm would come to her.

Next to his Inaugural portrait was her bottle of cooking sherry. So that's where she had left it!

Katie took another swig, whispered *I love you* to the president, and imagined him replying *I love you too, Katie.*

Katie was none too fond of Jackie. She sometimes said inane things, imitating Jackie's breathless voice.

"You sound ridiculous," Ralph told her. "Don't think about cutting a comedy album. Nobody will buy it."

She did love Caroline and John John. And now, they would soon have a baby brother or sister joining them in the White House. Which reminded Katie, she wanted to buy a gift for the new baby. Tomorrow she would have to check out some baby things. But for now, she went back to bed, hoping that Michelle would not be back in her dreams. Michelle had been banished. No one must speak of her, ever again. Not after what she did.

Let her be anathema! Bell, Book, and Candle. Out!

Thinking of Michelle at all was simply too much. No wonder Katie was always sick!

<h1 style="text-align:center;">CHAPTER 2</h1>

Dan Doyle went to the kitchen for a cup of coffee and noticed that the light was on in the Casey living room. He could not help but wonder why.

Perhaps it was Ralph. Oh, he could not stand Ralph Waldo Casey. What a literary name for such an ignoramus!

Ralph Casey was hardly one of his fans; he doubted that Ralph even read the label on a catsup bottle. Ralph was a bully, a braggart, and a loudmouth. To hear Ralph going on, you'd think the sun could not rise in the morning without consulting him first.

Or perhaps it was Dickie Casey, up to no good. Dickie was also the nickname Dan had given his cetacean anti-hero, Moby Dick II. He'd had that little monster in mind.

Dickie had been in some trouble last year. Dan had been working late at night and heard Brunhilde, the Wagner dachshund, barking. Her barking had a frantic quality. Dan peeked out and sure enough, there were teenage boys placing cherry bombs in mailboxes. The moon was full, and the ringleader stood underneath a street light. No question, it was Dickie, laughing his empty head off.

Dan had called the police. They arrived before Dickie could blow up his mailbox. Ralph was furious, not at his little Dickie but at those who would dare accuse him. Didn't they realize that Dickie was headed for college, then law school, then a political career? Wasn't there a seat in the Senate, waiting for Dickie?

God forbid, Dan thought.

Ralph had insisted the deed had been done by what he called those colored boys from the slums. Whatever. Dickie, being as white as his namesake, and from an affluent background, got off with a slap on the wrist. And a warning from the judge: "If I see you in my court again, Young Man, it won't go so well for you. Do I make myself clear?"

"Yes, Your Honor," Dickie squeaked in his not-dropped-yet voice.

Ralph never did believe in Dickie's guilt. Since then, he'd looked askance at Dan, suspecting he was the one who called the cops, as who else was up at that hour? But Ralph had already established himself in Dan's mind as a major pain in the rear.

Dan took his coffee back to his typewriter. It might have been Katie, up for some reason. One rarely saw Katie, even before what Dan called The Michelle Incident.

He thought back many years ago, when he had first moved into this house. He saw Katie walking down Muratori Boulevard with her two small children, Dickie and Michelle. He was reminded to two tugboats trying to guide a great ocean liner into the Port of New York.

The light in the Casey house went out. Just as well. Dan cranked another piece of paper into the typewriter and thought of Michelle. He remembered her singing in the Wagners' back yard.

Dan had been at a cookout at Hans and Frieda Wagner's place. They were refugees from the East side of the Berlin Wall. Terrific people, and Frieda had made her famous strudel.

Ralph was there with both his kids. Of course, there was no Katie. Even then she kept to herself. It was said, when the Casey family had first arrived, they were always being invited to cocktail parties and cookouts. Katie developed a pattern of sending an RSVP of yes. Or saying maybe. Then she would not show up at all. No one appreciates that.

Anyhow, Michelle was there with her guitar, singing that ticky-tacky song and everybody liked it, except for Ralph, who looked annoyed. Then he went back to yakking about how important he was. Michelle had come up to Dan.

"Mr. Doyle, can I ask you something?"

"Sure! As long as it's not about where I get my ideas!"

"Oh, no!"

"See, that's kind of like a leprechaun's pot o' gold." Dan had been a bit drunk; that he recalled.

"No, it's, well, I was wondering if I should take up writing. Like you do."

"You think you might want to?"

"I've thought about it, but Dad says I don't have any talent."

"Michelle, let me tell you something. Just between you and me. Your father is full of shit."

Michelle looked shocked but giggled.

"Look at him over by the pool!" Dan took a gulp of his drink. "Shooting off his mouth about how great he is. Yak, yak, yak. While Dickie just sits there with a hot dog rammed in his mouth, and a dumb expression on his face. Like he's someone the Kennedys would call *retaaded*. You think I'm falling for Ralphie Boy's act? Come on!

"See, Michelle, the trouble with people like me is, we make it look so easy and it's not. Writing is a hard life. You can have a load of talent and still get enough rejections to sink a battleship. You can't let them get you down. You will find out soon enough that a lot of the people you must deal with are, in fact, brass-plated bastards.

"I've met with people calling themselves agents and editors. Functionally illiterate! New York? A sewer. And, Hollywood? Let's not even go there. An exploding septic tank! Sheeeesh, the things that go on there!

"And even if your stuff gets published, things will go wrong. The Washington Post critic will say it stinks. Or it won't sell. Or you go on a trip to promote your book and nobody shows up. Or some screwball sues you, saying he thought of it first and you stole it.

"Or Hollywood makes a film of your book, only it's not like your book at all. They cast some dunce as your protagonist. You know the one I mean? I swear, he didn't change the expression on his face once, all during Battle of Gettysburg. He has a talent, all right, but it's not acting. It's something I won't mention in front of a refined young lady like yourself. Anyhow, these things happen."

"Really?" Michelle asked, wide-eyed.

"Look, Kid, I'll tell it to you straight. If you want to write, fine. Write a up a storm. But don't do it for money. Or fame. Or glory. Or to get your picture in the damn paper. Or to prove to your father that he's full of…you know. Write because it's what you want to do. Because you love it. Or don't bother. Remember, Kid, you go into this for the long haul. If you don't have the tenacity, the talent isn't worth a dime. Get me?"

"I think so."

Someone called Dan then, so he had to go. But not without giving Michelle one more tip: "Don't let your pop read your stuff. Keep your pearls away from swine."

"Oh, he never looks at anything I do. I got first prize for an essay I wrote at school. He never even looked at it."

"Just as well. If he's a literary critic, I'm Richard Nixon."

Shortly thereafter, Michelle left the neighborhood. She had won a scholarship to St. Ethel's Academy. What a big deal that was; one of the most exclusive schools you could imagine. Dan thought that Katie and Ralph would never stop bragging about it. But Dan had wondered, was it really such a good idea? Michelle was quiet and shy. Could she adapt to living with girls from such a different background?

Katie and Ralph never thought about that.

No more Michelle, Dan thought. Books, articles and stories unwritten. Songs unsung.

And it was such a damn shame.

CHAPTER 3

Dear Diary,

I suppose I have to start by saying hello. Hello out there! I'm Michelle Casey.

I go to T. S. Eliot High. Yes, that really is the name of my school. As the sign on the football field says, Welcome to T. S. Eliot, Home of The Hollow Men. And my English teacher says I'm supposed to be keeping a diary. This isn't an assignment. It's to help me express myself in writing. Not that I think anyone out there will actually read it. No one reads the thoughts of teenage girls unless they are Anne Frank or something. And I'm not nearly as interesting. Or unless they are the girls' brothers, trying to be nasty. I don't think mine will. He hates to read.

Yes, I have a brother. People call him Dickie. Never Dick, never Richard. Totally immature. Just like Dickie.

Dickie dresses like James Dean, although it drives Mom crazy. He speaks in grunts. He keeps his hair cut in a Duck's Ass, which Mom likes even less. And he uses too much of what the TV calls That Greasy Kid Stuff.

He never opens a book unless someone yells at him to read it and be prepared to discuss it in an intelligent manner. Hah! The only books he has no trouble reading are comic books. Batman. Superman. I've seen him read the Classic Comics version of real books, then write a book report. His teacher got wise to him. Even Mom and Dad were mad. They cracked down on Dickie. For a while. No more TV on school nights.

But it didn't last. It never does. Before long he was doing his homework in front of the TV again. Dad wants Dickie to go to law school, but all Dickie wants to be is Kookie on 77 Sunset Strip.

I don't have any other brothers or sisters. I have lots of cousins on my dad's side. He came from such a big family. And one on my mom's side. Steven Maldonato. I like him a lot. He's the opposite of Dickie, proof you can be totally cool and still get all As. If I had a choice of a brother, it would be Steve. But I don't.

I don't see Steve that much because his mother is my Aunt Claire. And Mom and Aunt Claire don't get along. Mom says Claire brought disgrace on this family by getting a divorce. But the fact is, Mom and Claire never got along, even when they were little.

However, I do talk to Aunt Claire and I really like her a lot. In fact, it's easier to talk to her than it is to Mom. Claire listens to me and takes me seriously. Mom just gets mad at everything and tells me not to do it. I don't think Claire is evil because she's divorced. She told me her ex-husband got obsessed with some crazy ideas, and that she and Steve were not safe around him. I think she did the right thing. I wish Mom would quit saying that Claire must think she's some movie star, because she doesn't.

I guess you could say I really don't get along that well with Mom. But she's very hard to satisfy. Nothing is ever good enough for her. Oh, and she thinks about the Kennedys, all the time. Like, if she were a Kennedy, she'd finally be happy. But I don't think she would be. She'd complain about the Secret Service. And because she's overweight, she would not look nearly as nice as Jackie does.

And then there's Dad and I've never had much of a relationship with him. He always pushes me aside and takes no interest in my school work. When I told him I made the honor roll, all he did was grunt. I don't think he even heard me. My report cards are supposed to be signed by both parents, but only Mom signs. Dad doesn't even look at it. Everything for him is Dickie, Dickie, Dickie. "Come on, Dickie, let's play ball. Let's have some fun!"

Let's see, what else can I tell you? I like school, I plan to go to college, but I'm not sure of what I want to be. I can play the guitar and sing like Joan Baez or Mary in Peter, Paul and Mary. (Only not when Dad's around. He says it gets on his nerves and calls it caterwauling.) Well, I'm not planning a career as a folk singer.

My neighbor across the street is Dan Doyle. He's always on the bestseller list. It would be great if I could write books like he does. I read all his books to see how he works out the plots. He really is a terrific person.

However, I don't think anyone is ever going to read this. Because, what have I got to say? I don't think I'm especially pretty or interesting. I have no boyfriend. I don't expect to have one. Unlike Dickie, I don't even date. And the fact is, I'm sad a lot of the time. Like, really sad. If I did not have to be in class, I might not get out of bed at all, some days. And when I hear Mom and Dad fighting, that makes it worse.

Then Mom gets mad because I won't smile and be pleasant. That's her key to everything: smile and be pleasant.

The only thing that helps is to go off somewhere and sing. Even if only birds and squirrels hear me.

Love, Michelle

****

Ask Not

Dear Diary,

Have you ever heard of St. Ethel's Academy? Neither did I, till a few days ago. It is a very expensive boarding school for girls with super rich parents. Only here is what they do: they offer scholarships for girls they see as having academic potential, as opposed to a ton of money.

But first, of course, you have to pass an entrance exam. There is a lot of competition. Mom found out about it. She wants me to take the exam.

I said I'd do it if it makes her happy. In Dad's words, I have all the chances of a snowball in Hell. He's probably right. I'm only doing this to get them to quit bugging me. I'm kind of worried that when the winner is announced, and it's someone else, they won't take it out on me.

This is just not realistic! But Mom says that if I win, it will open new doors for all of us. Well, especially for me. But Mom and Dad will be able to meet all the right people and go to all the right parties. Maybe even join a country club. Which makes no sense, Mom never goes to any parties around here, or does any entertaining. What does she expect of me? But lately she's been singing an old song to herself: We're in the Money. That gives me the creeps. Dad says that if I get in, I'll make the right connections. Marry the right guy. Who just might be Prince Charles. Please!

And, Dickie? Can you imagine him invited to the White House, wearing a tuxedo?

I think that if I did win, the only good thing would be that I'd live at St. Ethel's. I don't really like it here. Mom is always mad about something. If Kennedy has a press conference on TV, she's happy for a while, then goes back to being mad at someone. Usually Aunt Claire. And Dad, if he blows up, he's worse.

When he boils over, I hide in the closet. I'm afraid he's really going to hurt someone. And that person might be me. He's hit me and Dickie before. Now, Dickie's bigger than he is. He won't hit Dickie any more. But I'm less than half his size. And Mom always let him get away with it. And blames me. "You provoked him, Dear. Don't provoke him. Smile and be pleasant."

Sorry, Dear Diary, this is all so miserable. I want to take the exam and get it finished. Put it behind me. Who can blame me?

Love, Michelle

****

Dear Diary,

EEEEEKKKKK!

The exam results are back!

I won, I won, I WON!!!!!

I don't believe it! Mom and Dad are finally happy with me!

It's like in a poem Mr. Doyle read to me once. "The game is done! I've won! I've won! Quoth she, and whistles thrice."

I'm going to have to ask him the name of that poem. Meanwhile, three whistles for luck!

Love, Michelle

****

Dear Diary,

Things are so much better here. Last night Dad took us all out to Chez Francois to celebrate. I've never been in there before, it was like, wow! And Dad proposed a toast to me, actually called me the prettiest, smartest girl in the whole world, loud enough for everyone in the place to hear. He never said that before! And there was a cake for dessert in my honor.

Mom and I both had new dresses. Dickie didn't need a tuxedo, but he did have to wear a suit and tie. He looked ridiculous.

Tomorrow Mom, Dad and I are taking the train up to St. Ethel's for a tour of the campus. I'm getting really excited!

Love, Michelle

****

Dear Diary,

I am really worn out! The St. Ethel's campus is so big and I must have seen all of it. It's got everything. There's an indoor and outdoor pool, tennis courts, and some of the students are so rich, there's even a stable for their horses.

I even met one of the horses. He's a brown gelding name Whirlaway. I fed him an apple and I think he likes me. I like him!

First, though, I met the headmistress, Miss Emch, and several teachers. They seem nice and happy to see me. I didn't meet any other students, though, they were mostly in class. I did see the room where I will live. The view of the campus is spectacular.

For most of the tour, I kept trying to get away from Mom. She kept poking me and whispering, "Smile! Be pleasant!" I wish she'd give that a rest. Dad was asking Miss Emch questions like, who will Michelle get to know here? Do you have dances and parties? Are nice boys invited?

I was afraid he'd ask what the fathers of these nice boys do, and how much money they make. But I don't really care about that. When I asked Miss Emch, "Where is the library? Is it open on Saturdays?" Mom and Dad looked at me like they think I'm weird. But Miss Emch seemed pleased.

Well, I'm really tired out now. And kind of apprehensive. Some of the girls at T. S. Eliot, call St. Ethel's Snob Hill. I think a lot of them are jealous and don't want to be friends with me anymore. When I talked to Aunt Claire, it was like, "Are you sure you want to do this?"

But, yes. I am sure. I really think I can succeed in this. And I can't wait till September when I am out of this crazy house at last!

Love, Michelle

****

Dear Diary.

Well, here I am at St. Ethel's. I'm trying my best to fit in and I'm getting good grades. But something is not right here. It's not really what I expected at all.

We have an assembly before class every Monday morning. Miss Emch lectures us on St. Ethel's values and what we must represent to the outside world. We will be the leaders and the examples of society.

Honor. Honesty. Integrity. Miss Emch says these words more than Mom says, Smile and be pleasant. But they don't represent what I'm seeing.

St. Ethel's runs on an Honor Code. For instance, that means there are no proctors watching you during the exams. I've been through one set of exams and I was shocked at what went on. One girl had her open book in her lap. Cheat sheets were drifting around everywhere. So was copying. Elisabeth was trying to copy off me so I kept my hand over my paper. She said I'd be sorry.

Another thing about the Honor Code. There are no locks on our rooms. But things keep vanishing. Mom sent me a twenty-dollar bill. I put it on my bureau, stepped out, and it was gone. I've learned not to do that again.

I do not know why there is so much stealing going on. Anything these girls want; their parents will run right out and buy. They want for nothing. I can't imagine why they do this, or why no one in authority ever does anything about it.

And I've heard about other things, too. There are so many cliques here. (Not that I've been invited to join any of them.) But one clique takes the train to New York every weekend and shoplifts. Even though they know if they get caught, they get expelled. That hasn't happened yet.

Another girl was bragging that when she goes home, she dates married men, and they give her money and expensive presents.

I'm starting to agree with Aunt Claire. Maybe this was not such a good idea. But Mom and Dad insist that I stick it out till graduation. That's a long way off.

It's hard. I haven't made any friends yet, except Whirlaway. Because I'm on scholarship, no one takes me seriously. That's the hardest of all.

Love, Michelle

****

Dear Diary,

It's not getting any better.

Today, after class, I could see that someone had been in my room and moved my things around. Then I found out about Label Inspection. It's something Buffy van Hooper and her followers do to all new students. They go through your closets to make sure the labels in your dresses are from the finest stores. And I found out that when they saw my labels, they laughed. Sears. Montgomery Ward.

I'm worried because Buffy is so powerful on this campus. Her grandfather is the trustee who paid for the construction of the new gym. And her followers are only the most popular girls. There are times when I think that being at home was better than being here, even with Mom and Dad fighting. But if I ever mention that, they say it's out of the question. Absolutely I must not throw this chance away.

And smile. And be pleasant.

Love, Michelle

****

Dear Diary,

I had to go to the infirmary today. They tell me, I'll be all right, nothing broken, just take it easy for a few days and the bruise will fade.

During field hockey, Buffy rammed her stick into my shin. Really hard.

It hurt so much but the gym teacher saw it and said it was just an accident. So, don't worry about it. I'll try not to. At least winter break is coming up. I'm looking forward to it even if I have to be at home with Mom and Dad fighting.

Love, Michelle

Ask Not

****

Dear Diary,

Buffy had her Sweet Sixteen during winter break. There was a party at the Van Hooper estate in Westchester County. Buffy's followers made sure I found out about it, and that I was the only one in the class not invited. Her grandfather gave her a full-length mink coat for the occasion. It even has her initials, BVH, sewn into the lining.

Buffy was parading around the dorm, modeling it. She's going to be wearing it everywhere, even from class to class. Can you imagine being in high school and doing a thing like that?

I want to go back to T.S. Eliot High. I'm so unhappy here. Even Miss Emch spoke to me. She said she was pleased with my grades. But that I was being too shy and withdrawn and the others felt I was being unfriendly to them.

Me? Rejecting them?

I wish I could steal Whirlaway and ride away from this place. We could go someplace where no one knows either one of us, and start over. Even if they hang me as a horse thief, I'm starting to hate it!

Love, Michelle

****

CHAPTER 4

Katie felt better in the morning. There had been no more dreams. No John F. Kennedy, but on the other hand, no Michelle. And nothing featuring other people she could not stand: her sister Claire, to whom she was currently not speaking. Or her mother-in-law, Ma Casey, whom she could barely tolerate.

And, Ralph? He was getting difficult. Avocet had been Katie's maid for almost five years. That was the longest she ever had one maid. Avocet was the best: hard-working and reliable. But now, Ralph wanted to get rid of her.

"Why?"

"Because she costs too much as it is. And she's been dropping hints about a raise. Plus asking for other perks."

"We pay her practically nothing."

"Still. Too much. You can get another maid easily enough. Just run an ad in the *Clarion*. The phone will ring off the hook. You'll see. And ninety percent of them will be happy to work for less."

"Will they do a good job like Avocet? You know how I hate to iron. And how many maids did I have to go through, before I found one who didn't scorch your shirts? Just what perks has she been asking for? Maybe we can give them to her, instead of a raise."

"Uh-uh. Not what she wants. Time for her to go. By September, Avocet will be good and gone."

"But, Ralph…"

"You won't have to say a thing to her. Leave it all to me."

Katie had heard this song and dance act before. She would miss Avocet, but Ralph insisted, he knew what he was doing.

She decided to go to Bloomberry's Department Store. They were having a sale. Plus, they had such a nice baby department.

But what to buy? Pink or blue? There was no way to tell if Jackie Kennedy was having a boy or a girl. Not yet. Perhaps a more neutral color, so Katie could make her purchase and send it now.

That yellow ensemble with the tiny feet was just adorable. Katie purchased it, then had it sent to the White House with a card saying, with love to Baby, from Katie Casey. She was quite pleased with herself.

Ralph, however, was not. "Jeez, Katie, why did you have to go and do that?"

"I wanted the new baby to have something nice!"

"It's a Kennedy! It's not going to be wearing hand-me-downs! It's probably got too much stuff already. And just what did this cost, anyway?"

Katie refused to answer. "Well, Ralph, I'm sorry you feel that way," was all she would say. Katie went up to her room and shut the door. Ralph could be so obtuse. He stood outside the bedroom door, nagging.

"How much did you blow on this? Katie, you don't even know these people. And they don't even know you! What, you think you're one of them, or something? You think if you went to Hyannis Port, they'd let you in the compound? Katie?"

She said nothing.

"You wish you were Jackie? What a laugh! You'd redecorate the White House with this crap you buy on sale?"

Katie put the pillow over her head.

"Which Kennedy to you think you are, anyway?" Ralph paused and asked, "The fat one? I've got a piece of news for you, Katie, there aren't any fat ones! So, you might as well....Katie?"

No response.Katie pulled the pillow off and pounded it with her fist.

Ralph droned on. "Because you're really going too far with this Kennedy business. Jack Kennedy does not want anything from you, but your vote. He got it. He will get it next year. End of story. He doesn't even know who you are. Neither does he care!

"You think about them all the time. And it's not good, Katie. It's not healthy. Maybe you ought to talk to somebody about it, I don't know."

Katie heaved the pillow at the door.

Is he calling me crazy? How dare he say such a thing! Katie's cheerful mood was ruined. Talk to somebody? Like a psychiatrist? As if she would ever need one! What a disgrace, to do such a thing!

Ralph was going to get the silent treatment, and he'd get it for a good long time.

CHAPTER 5

Dan was having his morning coffee on the front porch. He observed Ralph walking down the driveway. As Ralph got into this car, Dickie ran up to him.

"Dad?"

"Yeah?"

"Mom says to pick up a loaf of Wonder Bread and a quart of milk on your way home."

"Yeah? Well, if she wants 'em that bad, she can damn well tell me herself!" Ralph drove off.

Dan had to snicker. He imagined a place where he had never been and would probably never go: the Casey living room.

All the upholstery was covered in plastic. The décor was Early Pat Nixon. Republican. Sensible. Hideous. The three Caseys were seated in a circle.

Katie would turn to Dickie and say, tell your father blah-blah. Ralph would then turn to Dickie and say, oh, yeah? You tell your mother blah-blah!

At least it was keeping Dickie out of trouble. But the atmosphere on Saturn must be more breathable than the one in that house.

Dan got up and poured the rest of his coffee into the shrubbery. He really needed to get back to Moby Dick II. He had already wasted enough time on the phone with George.

Oh, George? George was his half-brother from Peoria who had stayed with him during the Michelle incident. That George.

But his editor was getting antsy about his protagonist, the brave able-bodied Seaman Charlie Ahab. Charlie's ancestor had nailed a Spanish gold coin to the mast of the *Pequod*. That was the reward for the sailor who first spotted the original Moby Dick. However, it was said that the coin contained a talisman against the white whale. Thus, the wreckage of the *Pequod* had to be found and raised to the surface. Dan's editor needed to know how the Hell Charlie intended to do this. It was still a mystery to Dan.

Still, once he started remembering Michelle, he could not stop. The first shock came on a day when many strangers were seen going in and out of the Casey house. Police cars were parked on Grimlkyn Lane. Then Ralph came out of his house, disheveled and reeking of alcohol.

"Michelle's dead," he announced.

There were gasps of *no, impossible, can't be, not Michelle!*

"All she wanted to do was take bath. She tripped, hit her head on the faucet, went head-first in the tub and drowned."

Inside the house, something shattered. Dan heard Katie scream, "You are no sister of mine if you do that! I will never speak to you again!"

A woman who looked like a thin version of Katie stormed out the door and shouted, "That suits me fine!" She left so fast her tires made a rubber imprint on the street.

There was the next shock, when Ralph announced that there would be no viewing, no funeral service, no flowers, no notice in the Clarion obituaries, no nothing. Dan remembered thinking: *something is not adding up here. Their only daughter dies in a tragic accident, and this is what they do? Something is very off here.*

Two days later came the worst shock of all. There was a letter in Dan's mailbox, on St. Ethel's elegant stationery. *"Dear Mr. Doyle,"* Michelle wrote. *"By the time you get this, I will be dead."*

Dan had to sit down.

"I have to leave St. Ethel's in the morning," Michelle wrote. *"Mom and Dad are going to take me home and they are furious with me. Especially Dad. I can't face them. I really let everyone down. I tried my best, but the headmistress says my presence here is too disruptive. These rich girls don't want me around. I'm going to end my life tonight. I gave this a lot of thought, and I am certain of my decision. I kept a diary and sent it to Aunt Claire. You were a good friend to me and I thank you for that. Love, Michelle. PS: You can show this to Aunt Claire if you want. Please don't show it to Mom, Dad or Dickie."*

There was no way in Hell Dan would show the letter to Mom, Dad or Dickie. In her haste to end her life, Michelle had forgotten to provide Aunt Claire's last name, address or phone number. Claire who?

With the help of a few of the other housewives on the block, Dan had been able to track Claire down. Frieda Wagner was the most helpful. Katie had told her once that she had a sister Claire in Silver Hill Park, whom she rarely saw. Apparently, they never did care for each other. They found a Claire Quinn at that location, in the phone book.

"Quinn, *Ja,*" Frieda said. "I think that was Katie's maiden name."

Dan dialed the number, afraid to upset her even more. But Claire remembered him well. "You signed my copy of *The Silver Troika* at Brentano's. I could not put it down."

"Well, thank you, but..." Dan then had to explain about the letter Michelle had sent him.

There was a long pause and then, "My Lord. That poor girl."

"She, um, mentioned a diary?"

"Yes, yes, I did get it. And it does mention you in several places, she thought so highly of you."

Dan and Claire agreed to meet at Claire's place. She did not want to go to Dan's.

"I swear, if I did, I might have to look at that so-called sister of mine. No funeral, no service at all? How could she do that, to her own daughter? If I see her, I'm going to slap that fat face of hers."

"Ah, yes, Miss Quinn." The last thing Dan needed was to try and break up a cat fight.

"I'll tell you all about her when you get here. I'll tell you plenty! And about that troglodyte she married, too. They deserve each other."

Dan recognized Claire as the woman who had left the Casey house in a rage. Claire recognized Dan from the back cover of The Silver Troika.

"I swear, Mr. Doyle…"

"Please. Just Dan."

"I swear, Dan, I am so mad I could chew nails and spit tacks. No service? No way to say good-bye to my niece? Does that sound right to you?"

"You're so upset."

"Well, who wouldn't be? I gave them both a piece of my mind. And then I told them…."

Claire paused for breath. "I'm having a priest friend of mine, Father Gray, say a Mass for Michelle. You must have heard of him. He's always getting in the papers, kind of radical, the one in trouble with the cardinal?"

"Yes, but was Michelle even Catholic?"

"Michelle and that Dickie were both baptized as babies, so yes, she was, legally. Even though her parents never took her back inside a church again. And when I told my banshee sister I'd do that, what did she say? 'If you do that, I will never speak to you again!' Hah. Small loss, I say."

"And your friend has no problem with the cause of death?"

"You mean, that it was suicide? No. After all the poor girl went through? I let him look at Michelle's diary. Here it is. She'd want you to see it. But let me tell you what that Ralph tried to pull! He wanted to medical examiner to falsify the death certificate. To show the cause of death as an accidental drowning. The medical examiner had Ralph thrown out of his office."

"Good for the medical examiner!"

"Oh. One other thing. This Mass will be next Friday at eleven AM in the basement chapel at St. Mary Magdalen."

"I'd be honored to be there," Dan promised her.

Dan then opened the diary. *Tolle, lege.* Take up and read. He started with Michelle's last entries at St. Ethel's.

****

Dear Diary,

Buffy's mink coat is missing. I was trying to figure out, who would be so bold as to steal from her? Everyone seems upset about it. But things are much worse for me now.

Buffy went to Miss Emch and filed an Honor Code Violation, claiming that I stole her coat.

I swear I would never do such a thing!

But now it's such big deal and I have to go through an investigation. I'm so humiliated. I know Buffy wants me gone but this is really going to an extreme. I can't tell Mom and Dad; they'd be furious. And the others think I'm guilty, that I already sold it for thousands of dollars, which I hid in a Swiss bank account. Which I don't have! What can I do?

Love, Michelle

****

Dear Diary,

The investigation is over. Miss Emch found out that not only did I not steal Buffy's coat, it was impossible for me to have done so.

As for the coat, it's back. I suspect that Buffy knew where it was all along. But I can't say anything.

I guess I feel sorry for Miss Emch, she's been trying to come up with a way to rein in Buffy without involving her grandfather. Which is not possible. But Buffy still wants me gone, she's claiming my presence on campus is too disruptive. I feel like I'm a drop of blood in a shark tank. I can't study for mid-terms. I can't stop crying.

Love, Michelle

****

Dear Diary,

Miss Emch has decided on what to do. I'm not getting expelled from St. Ethel's. Instead, I'm going to quietly drop out and go home.

It's over.

Miss Emch is concerned about my state of mind, so she's sending me home with a referral to Dr. Taylor. He specializes in teenage depression.

But he's a psychiatrist. Mom will never permit me to see one of those. And Dad will never pay for it.

They're supposed to pick me up Saturday morning. They may act like they're calm about it, but the minute we get home, they are going to rip me up. Especially Dad. Their high society dreams are over. They will never be listed in the Social Register, or on the White House guest list. Mom will never be presented to John F. Kennedy. It's my fault.

And I can't do it; I can't face them.

Dear Diary, this is my final entry. On Friday, I am going to mail you to Aunt Claire along with a letter to Mr. Doyle.

Then I'm going to the stable to say good-bye to Whirlaway.

Then I'm going to end my life. I'm going to fill the bath tub up with water, get in, and open my wrists with a razor blade.

I want to apologize to anyone who is hurt by this. Especially Grandma Casey who took such good care of me, and called me Mimi.

I'm trapped! There is no other way out and I can't take it anymore!

Love, Michelle

****

"God have mercy," Dan said, closing the diary. He felt his palms grow wet and his stomach lurched.

"If it's any comfort to you," Claire told him, "on Saturday, when Ralph and Katie were there to take her home, there was a search of the campus. No sign of Michelle. It was this Buffy who broke into the bath tub stall and found Michelle's body. It's said that to this day, she's still screaming."

"Hmm," said Dan. "Buffy sounds awfully good at breaking and entering, doesn't she?"

"I noticed."

"I hope she lives one hundred years and never stops seeing that. And that she screams forever in Hell."

"I agree."

Dan and Claire met again at the Mass for Michelle. He took George with him. George, of course, his half-brother from Peoria. There was no Ralph, Katie or Dickie. Dan remembered one old lady, Ralph's mother, several Casey brothers and cousins, and students and teachers from T. S. Eliot High. That was all. A pity and a damned disgrace.

Eternal rest grant unto her, O Lord, and let perpetual light shine upon her. May Michelle Casey and the souls of all the faithful departed rest in peace. Amen.

"Amen to that," Dan told himself, and went back to his typewriter. He'd have Claire out to lunch sometime soon. They had become friends, so one good thing came out of the tragedy.

They helped each other through the loss. Dan took Claire out for spins in the Porsche. He could make Claire laugh by telling her true stories about Hollywood.

And if Ralph and Katie were still fighting, let them nuke each other flat, for all Dan cared. He cranked another piece of paper into his typewriter and got back to Moby Dick II, who had the entire US Navy in an uproar.

At the same time Ralph was thinking, maybe all of this had to come to a stop.

Katie would never agree to a divorce. If he filed for one, she'd fight it tooth and nail. Look at the way she dumped on Claire for being divorced.

But it might shake her up a bit if, say, she got a letter from someone claiming to be Ralph's attorney. It would inform her that if she did not stop this silent treatment, divorce proceedings would begin. It just might be worth a try.

Or, maybe, while she was lying in bed, get out his suitcase, throw in a few things, then slam the front door hard as he walked out. That would speak volumes without words. Katie wants the silent treatment? He'd give it back to her.

He recalled how it all started.

He stood at the altar with his best man, his brother Paul, and his other groomsmen. They included the Casey brothers except for Father (later Bishop) Casey, who would preside.

Why am I doing this?

The organ thundered Here Comes the Bride. First the ring bearer and the flower girl, tiny Casey cousins, processed up the aisle to a chorus of awwwwws. Then the bridesmaids, in size places, the shortest first.

Then Katie, on the arm of Mr. Quinn.

Whose idea was this?

Katie had always been substantial, even though she was not yet obese. Her shiny white gown emphasized her weight. She was followed by a train long enough to require a train-bearer.

"Dearly Beloved, we are gathered here…" Father Casey began.

The memory jumped ahead to the reception in the Grand Ballroom at the Ritz. No expense had been spared. There was even a live band, and God only knew what that cost. Then it was time for their first dance as Mr. and Mrs. Ralph Casey. It was like dancing with a loaded Mack dump truck.

One the dance floor was open for the guests, Ralph caught sight of Claire dancing with a sailor to the Big Band classic, *In the Mood*. And could they ever cut the rug! They could give Fred and Ginger some serious competition.

Katie was seething at her sister. Claire was outshining the bride.

Ralph wished he could give Claire a spin around the floor. But no, Katie would never stand for it. The last thing he wanted was fight on his wedding night. Still, he felt a pang of regret.

He should have gone after Claire, the pretty sister. Too late now; he was a married man.

Another jump ahead, to the birth of Dickie. He'd been a big baby, ten pounds at least, and Katie never did lose that baby weight before starting….

Before starting Michelle. Despite Dickie's size, he'd come out quickly. Michelle was a tiny little thing, and in a breech position. Her delivery was long and hard. Katie developed some sort of condition. She had to stay in the hospital even after Michelle could go home. Ma Casey had to move in to care for the new baby.

"I think I can do this!" Ma reminded him. "Sure, and didn't I raise all eight of you?"

Ma was so crazy about Baby Michelle. Instead of Lullaby and Good Night, she'd sing her a Maurice Chevalier song about Mimi. Her pretty little Mimi.

Ralph was dazed and confused. He was certain this second child would be a boy, that his home would be like the one he grew up in: overrun with rough and tumble boys. The notion that he would be responsible for a girl was incomprehensible to him. He'd been reading a lot in the papers about these flying saucers. Were they really from outer space? Manned by strange creatures? It was as if one of them landed in his yard, and Michelle crawled out.

Ralph had never felt as close to her as he did to Dickie. Dickie was the son with whom he could wrestle and take to the football games. And he'd wanted more sons, more Dickies. But when Katie came home from the hospital, she still wasn't well. Her doctor had advised against any more babies.

Instead of losing the baby weight, Katie started gaining more and more. Her blood pressure zoomed up. She remained in bed as long as she could, like the queen of a termite colony. Ma Casey did the feeding, diaper changes, housework and laundry. Plus, Ma had to deal with

Dickie, who was jealous, acting up, and had forgotten his toilet training.

Finally, the arrangement had to be terminated although Katie said she was still sickly. "Have you noticed?" she asked Ralph. "When your mother picks up Michelle, she giggles. When I pick her up, what happens? *Waah!* Michelle will have to learn who her real mother is."

Ma never complained about it. What Ma did complain about was that when she finally left, she got not one word of thanks from Katie.

"Who does she think she is?" Ma had asked Ralph. "The Duchess of Windsor? Who are we, her footmen and ladies in waiting?"

"Ma, please, Katie's had a hard time and not been well."

"It might help her to shed those extra tons."

It was true. Katie had taken Ma's hard work for granted. No wonder they didn't get along.

Would Ma be glad if he got rid of Katie? There was no telling. He'd be the only divorced Casey brother. Not good.

Ralph would not go through with this. But he had to show Katie the consequences of her actions, and hope she didn't call his bluff.

CHAPTER 6

Ralph arrived home on a hot day in August, fed up as usual. His shirt was soaked with sweat. Katie still would not speak to him except through Dickie.

She was about to get an official looking letter from someone he knew. Attorney at Law. (Grass cut, leaves raked, snow removed.)

As he pulled into the driveway he noticed the window air conditioner in the living room was at full blast. No doubt, no one was in the living room. There was more of his money down the drain.

He entered the house through the back door to the kitchen. There was Dickie, gazing into the refrigerator, lost in contemplation of its contents. Not only was the living room empty, the TV had been left on, too.

"Will you shut that damn thing? And how many times have I told you to turn the air conditioner off when you're not in the living room?"

"Well, Gee, Dad…"

"Well, Gee, nothing! I'm sick of these sky-high electric bills!"

Dickie took the hint and shut the refrigerator.

"What's for dinner?" Ralph asked.

"I don't know."

"Well, where's your mother?"

"In her room."

"Great, she hasn't even started dinner yet?"

"No."

"So where does that leave us? My mother's place? Or the damn diner? Let's go."

"Um, Dad, I don't know if you heard it on the news."

"Heard what? I've been stuck in these stupid meetings all day!"

"Mom's kind of upset because Jackie Kennedy had her baby."

"Wait a minute. Her baby's not due, not yet."

"That's it. The baby's way too early."

"Did it live?"

"Yeah. Last I heard, it's alive. But something's wrong. It doesn't look good. Mom kind of flipped out."

Ralph grunted. "Boy or girl, did they say?"

"Boy."

"That's a shame. Everybody wants a boy."

"Patrick Bouvier Kennedy."

"Nice name. Irish and French. Damn shame."

"You know how Mom feels, she sent him a present and everything."

"Yeah, yeah, I know. I'll just have to go on up. See if I can get through to her."

Katie was flopped across the bed, sobbing.

"Honey?" Ralph asked.

She said nothing.

"Look…um, I heard, and I know this is hard. But you know, the kid might be all right? Haven't they got him in one of those incubators?"

"Ralph, he's so tiny." At least she was back to speaking to him.

"Yeah, well, they got those incubators, and a lot of those kids who get born too early, they turn out all right." Ralph paused. "Don't they?"

He thought of his brother Liam's son, who was premature and survived, but turned out to be totally blind. He decided against mentioning that.

"He can hardly breathe. He can't cry like a normal baby. Ralph, what can I do?"

"What can you do? I'll tell you, Katie. Nothing. There is nothing you can do at all, so…"

Katie sniffled. "Poor, poor Jackie! I'll never say anything nasty about her again!"

"Maybe it's best if you don't." Again, he could not add that they were both mothers of lost children.

"My baby. My sweet baby boy Patrick."

"Hold it, hold it, Katie, what did you just say?"

Katie shook her head.

"You said, *my* baby, Katie. My baby Patrick. My, get it? Katie, he is not your baby! You didn't carry him. He is not Claire's baby, your best friend's baby, your next-door neighbor's baby. *Not yours!* Not in any way! Now, it's sad, but this happens every day, babies come out before they're ready. And a lot of them don't survive."

Katie sobbed.

"This happens! Do you act like this over every single one?"

"No."

"All right, then! Pull yourself together."

"I'll pray. I'll say a rosary."

For a moment, Ralph did not know what to say. He and Katie were Catholic in name only. Katie had never been known to pray about anything, not even Michelle.

"OK, you do that, if it makes you happy."

"Ralph, where is my rosary?"

"Damned if I know! Did you ever even have one?"

"It's around here somewhere." Katie pulled open a drawer in the night stand.

"Suit yourself," Ralph said. "But, Honey, I want you to think about this. Patrick What's-his-name Kennedy is not your baby. I know you like the Kennedys, but this is way over the top. You're over-reacting."

Katie said nothing, but kept rooting around in the drawer, for the one item she would never find there. There was Ralph's loaded handgun which he kept ready in case anyone broke in.

"Careful, Honey, don't touch that. You know I keep it loaded with the safety off."

But there was nothing that resembled a rosary.

CHAPTER 7

Dan and Claire met at a sidewalk café downtown. They lit their cigarettes, two on a match, and ordered iced tea and scones.

"I've been thinking about that Kennedy baby," Claire admitted. "What a fight he put up! Brave little fellow. What a president he would have made for the twenty-first century."

Claire took a puff. "His father's trying to get us to the moon. Patrick would have taken us to Mars. And beyond."

"Some things just aren't meant to be. Poor little guy, never had a chance."

Dan thought of one of his plot devices. He'd foreshadow a major event by creating a similar one an as omen. If this was some sort of omen, it was not a good one. But of what, he could not imagine.

"Oh, I met Frieda Wagner at Food Fair. She told me why Katie and Ralph are having their own Cold War."

"Do tell, I'm all ears!"

"Katie bought a gift for the Kennedy baby and sent it to the White House without telling Ralph in advance. That did not go over big with Mr. Cheapskate."

"And why would anyone named Kennedy, need anything from Katie Casey?"

"It's a funny thing. You know, I get all of this third-hand. But Katie, it seems, has gotten obsessed with the Kennedys." Another puff. "It could well be, she's in love with Jack or Bobby."

"Hey, why not throw in Teddy?"

Claire laughed. "And Ralph hasn't got a clue. But you know him. Like two of the Three Wise Monkeys. He sees and hears only what he wants. Good or evil. But, wow, can he speak evil!"

Their lunch was served. "Dig in!" Claire advised him.

Claire was no longer Miss Quinn to Dan; she was just plain Claire. "I used to be Miss Quinn," she had said, "then for a while I was Mrs. Maldonato. Then I went back to being Miss Quinn."

"Divorced?"

"Yep."

"I'm sorry."

"Don't be. It was in everyone's best interest. As for what went wrong: three words: John Birch Society."

"You mean the right-wing weirdos?"

"When I married Will, he was a pretty decent guy. In fact, we both worked on the Democratic campaign in '56. Then Will changed, he really went gung-ho for this extremist stuff. I just don't know. I even went to their meetings, trying to understand. But it got to the point where I could not take any more of it. So, I told him, and I got a black eye in return."

"What a creep!" Dan said.

"Well, I didn't want him around me or our son Steven any more. So, I filed for divorce. Katie didn't like it at all and sided with Will. 'A divorce in our family. What a disgrace. A woman alone can't survive, especially not with a child. You will both end up on welfare.' That's what she said. I became a speech therapist. I work with people who have had strokes. I give them back their voices. And I think I've done all right for myself."

"And Steven?"

"He's a midshipman, Class of '65. Way up near the top of his class. He sings tenor in the choir. I'm so proud of him I could explode. But you know how Ralph is, he compares my son to his little Dickie-Poo, and he gets jealous. That's Ralph for you."

"Ever think of getting married again?"

"Pfui."

Claire had told Dan so many things about herself. She was an amazing woman, way ahead of her time. As for Dan, his own autobiography was already well known. Dan's father was dead, his mother lived in Mineola. He had two ex-wives, one in Alaska, the other in India, seeking enlightenment. And four kids, being educated in Swiss schools. Oh, and there was George, his half-brother from Peoria.

The scones in this place were great, always so fresh. "You know it's kind of strange," Dan said. "You and Katie are sisters, brought up together, and you turned out so different."

"Well, it happens. You already told me so much about Hollywood."

"It's a factory town. You know they manufacture illusions and people pay for them."

"I'd say this about my growing up with Katie. It was a lot like one of my favorite films: *Mildred Pierce*."

"My God! One of my all-time favorites, too! Wasn't Joan Crawford magnificent? Did you know that got her an Oscar?"

"Oh, yeah. My childhood was not really like the film. Our mother was no Mildred. Oh, she was in the kitchen all the time and wow, could she cook and bake! And didn't Katie love it! But it never occurred to Mom to work outside the home, much less start her own business. Or get divorced. Nope, Katie and I were like Mildred's daughters."

"Veda and Kay."

"You got it. I was Kay: good natured, a bit tomboyish, always dancing up a storm. Unlike Kay, though, I did not die as a child. I could have, though."

"How come?"

"Polio."

"Oh, no!"

"I managed to do without the iron lung, thank God. Made a full recovery. But I don't really remember much of it. Just being sick and miserable in the hospital. Anyhow, I was Kay, and Katie was Veda."

"How I would love to haul off and slap that Veda. Selfish, conniving, using everyone else in her path. Including her own mother."

"Katie was like that from her first day. A little queen. She had our parents wrapped around that plump finger of hers. She even made household rules: Our folks were not allowed to go into Bloomberry's, unless they came out with a present for her. And if it was not up to her standards, back it went, followed by days of whining."

"Funny, then, that she married Ralph."

"Not really. He asked her, and her goal was to have a wedding worthy of a Radio City spectacle. She had to have all the bells and whistles. Plus, an article on the Clarion's society page. Dad made sure she got it. Dad had some guilt issues. My parents' marriage was not happy. Long story short. But as for Katie, she wanted her Big Wedding, and I really don't think she gave much of a damn, who the groom was."

"Or, what happens next."

Claire laughed out loud. "No, I don't think that even occurred to her! Surprise! But, seriously, even then, she and I were on the outs. She had ten bridesmaids and I was not even one of them."

"That's mean."

"I was treated like one of the poor relations, barely tolerated. And you know something, Dan? I didn't care. I still don't. I would have been embarrassed to be a part of something so tacky."

Claire lit another cigarette. "This Wedding of the Century was going to be Katie's entrée into high society."

"Ralph is hardly among the elites."

"Yeah, but remember, he's so full of bull. Katie may well have fallen for it. Only later did she learn about his vulgarity. He'll never fit in with the jet set. But that didn't stop her from feeling she was destined for a life better than the one she had. And she's always had such a rich fantasy life."

"Hence, her obsession with the Kennedys."

"Plus, the whole Irish Catholic thing, being made to feel like an outsider, wanting so badly to be an insider. You remember, during the Depression? There really were signs: Help Wanted. Irish Need Not Apply. But now she's the queen, and her home is her castle."

"What about Ralph? Isn't he the king of the castle?"

Claire shook her head, no. "He may think he is. At best, he's the prince consort, staying a step behind her when she opens Parliament. Or whatever the Hell her royal duties are. And when the queen banishes you, you stay banished. Forever."

They both sat silent with the memory between them. Michelle. Then Claire spoke that name.

"Michelle and I used to be close. Katie wasn't happy about that. She thought I was a bad influence, being divorced. Before Michelle went to St. Ethel's, she'd tell me things, what really went on in the castle. Ralph had been telling everybody that Dickie could go to any college he wanted. Even the Ivies were fighting over him. But Michelle told me that Dickie had applied to only one. Whitmoor. Hardly Ivy League, more of a *meh*. Whitmoor rejected Dickie right off the bat."

"Did Michelle know why?"

Claire crushed out her cigarette. "You bet she did. Ralph left the rejection letter on the coffee table. It had nothing to do with Dickie's grades or his SAT scores, which were both *meh*. No, it said that Dickie was felt to be too immature for a college experience."

"About time somebody told him that."

"But Michelle was frightened. Ralph was running amok through the house, screaming that he was going to sue Whitmoor College for a million dollars. Michelle did not want to be anywhere around him when he got all out of control like that."

"Such a vulnerable girl."

"Absolutely. What did she say? Blood in the shark tank. That's why I did not see this chance to put her in St. Ethel's as an opportunity. More of a disaster, lurking on the horizon.

I should have done more research about these girls from modest backgrounds, going there on scholarship. How many survived till graduation? Not many, I think. Still, Katie was crowing all over town about it. Finally, she'd get into the right circles, thanks to Michelle. And when Michelle was crushed under the weight of that burden…"

Dan added: "Her Majesty banished Michelle."

Claire nodded. "There's nothing in the castle to show that Michelle ever existed. Her Majesty's loyal subjects are forbidden to speak Michelle's name. I stand up for Michelle, and I'm banished, too. Well, as far as I'm concerned, this whole damn royal family can go screw itself."

"I miss Michelle so much. Her guitar, her funny little songs. I almost wish there were a way for the peasants to revolt."

"There's not. But it seems to me…" Claire paused. "It seems to me that their castle is built on top of an earthquake fault. And when it hits…."

"When it hits, and the whole damn castle turns out to made not of stone, but of ticky-tacky, down it goes."

"That's the advantage of our being in exile. We don't go down with it."

CHAPTER 8

Dan needed to spend some time in Los Angeles, and by the time he got back, it was clear that summer was on its way out. He did like to rake his leaves himself as he sang *The Banana Boat Song.*

Daylight come and me want go home.

The only downside was, Ralph was also raking, pausing every few minutes to glare at Dan. But, why? Dan felt Ralph was looking for something for which he could be blamed. For instance, Ralph might start complaining that Dan was neglecting his house, lowering everyone else's property values. In fact, Dan's house was the best-looking on the block. He kept it freshly painted in subdued colors and had even added a sunroom out back. What was the problem? Jealousy again?

I work all night on a drink of rum.

And where was Dickie on this fine Fall day? A window in the Casey house was open and the TV was on loud enough for Dan to hear a football game in progress. Dickie loved football. He did not play. He never even tried out for the T. S. Eliot Hollow Men team. He sat on the sofa and vegetated, while watching others play.

Briefly, Katie came out of the house and spoke to Ralph. So, they had agreed to a cease-fire.

Hide de deadly black tarantula.

Katie was wearing a truly ugly housedress, pink with garish yellow flowers. Her hair, which had not seen a comb in a while, was sticking out all over her head. She had gained even more weight.

"Hmmm. Her color's not good. Katie does not look well. Not at all."

"It's just getting worse and worse," Katie complained. "There's a mountain of ironing, and I just can't face it. And all that dust on the furniture, and dirt ground into the carpet. I'm overwhelmed. And all Dickie ever does is make a worse mess. He leaves those sticky Coke bottles all over the place. That sort of thing attracts roaches."

"Didn't you hire a new maid?"

"I've had three of them since you got rid of Avocet."

"Avocet quit, remember?"

"Avocet did no such thing."

"Yes, she did. She would not accept what we pay her, so she decided on her own to leave with no reference, nothing to say for the past five years, and good riddance if that's what makes her happy."

"I don't know what you did, Ralph, but this is not working out. I've had three maids. I've told you what the problems were, and you did not listen. One was on the phone all day. One had no idea of how to iron. She burned a hole right through an expensive shirt. And the third never showed up at all. That's all I can get for what you are willing to pay."

"All right, Katie! I'll help you. I'll run the vacuum or something."

"When?"

"When I'm done with this! Unless you want to rake?"

Katie gave him a dirty look, went back into the house, and shouted at Dickie that he was the laziest thing that ever drew breath.

Frieda Wagner strolled by, walking Brunhilde. Dan paused to pet the dachshund. Shortly thereafter, a few others from down the block walked up the sidewalk on Ralph's side. They spoke with Ralph and Dan heard the words, *your daughter.*

Ralph was forbidden to utter Michelle's name in his wife's presence. But Katie was out of earshot. Ralph dropped his leaf rake and told these people Michelle's story. Rather, his version of Michelle's story.

"What a tragedy!" Ralph was saying. "All she wanted to do was take a bath, she tripped, fell in head first, and drowned! Oh, she was so beautiful, so brilliant and talented!"

"How terrible!" his listeners agreed.

"You know, I'm going to sue St. Ethel's. For a million dollars."

"Good luck with that!"

At least he was getting his share of sympathy. But Dan knew it was a lie. Every word of it. Dan had to go back into his own house, rather than hear any more of those maudlin lies.

Many times, Dan had heard Ralph snapping at Michelle. He'd ask her what she wanted to do and he say, "Oh, no! You don't have the brains, the sense, the talent, the looks, to do that!"

"Everything she said, he belittled, Dan thought to himself. Now that she's dead, she's so smart, talented, beautiful! You'd think she was Miss Universe. Ralph, you are a jerk and a half, and you're milking this for all it's worth. You must have no shame at all."

Dan poured himself a drink.

"And now he's going to sue St. Ethel's? I just bet he is. Based on what? His lie about a hazardous bath tub? If he filed suit based on the truth, he might have a crack at winning. But there's no way Ralph will go ahead with a lawsuit. The mere thought of St. Ethel's legal defense team would send Ralph running the other way."

Dan thought of T. S. Eliot's The Wasteland.

"Fear death by water."

But Michelle did not drown! That was a damn lie! The copy of the report Claire had showed that Michelle's head leaned on the edge of the tub, nowhere near the water line.

"Oh, well, it's a wasteland. It's all a vast wasteland we live in. And not just TV."

In Los Angeles, Dan had gone on a bar crawl with his attorney. Now there was a man who knew all the right people. Jack Kennedy's actor brother-in-law, Peter Lawford. His former friend, Frank Sinatra. He ran with the entire Rat Pack. And once the whiskey had loosened up his tongue, he had so much to say.

"Talk about this town being an illusion factory? You got a point there, Danny Boy. And we all work the assembly line. What you see is rarely what you get."

"How so?" Dan had asked.

"You want an example? I got one for you. Ladies and Gentlemen, the President of the United States!"

"What about him?"

"What do people believe about him? Family man all the way, devout Roman Catholic."

"What are you getting at? Are you saying he's running around on Jackie?"

"No."

"All right, then."

"He's setting speed records! Ought to be in the Olympics!"

"You're shitting me."

"I swear it, Danny. No shit."

"With who?"

"For starts: the late, lamented, Marilyn Monroe."

"My God!"

"To lapse into legalese, Marilyn Monroe et al. And that et al part is quite a lot." His attorney shook the ice cubes in his Scotch. "He never hears the word no. Or, I'm married. Or, you're married. Big stars. Pretty starlets. Stars' secretaries. In the immortal words of the immortal Julius Caesar, Vidi, Vici, Veni. That's in Latin. Means: he saw, he conquered, he came. I'm sure you get my meaning."

"Incredible! Suppose word of this gets out? Before the '64 election?"

"It won't, Danny me boy. The illusion factory won't let it. But let me tell you…oh, to be in his shoes, if only for a day! I could die a happy man. And I bet you could, too."

That had offered Dan plenty of food for thought. Wouldn't it be funny, if it were true and Katie found out? She'd never believe it, though.

But the illusions went on. And Dan, truth be told, would not want to be in Kennedy's shoes. He had his own illusions. He hated maintaining them, but he had no choice.

His two ex-wives and four children did not exist, any more than Moby Dick II did. And, George? His half-brother from Peoria? George was only his middle name, they were not related, and he was not from Peoria.

It was George who meant the whole world to him.

They could not risk having the outside world know the truth about them. George worked for one of the big utilities. He could lose his job. Dan was self-employed, but still, supported by his vast number of fans. Were they ready to know this?

Probably not.

It was getting dark now, too late to finish raking. Dan locked his rake back in the shed and was pleased to see Ralph gone. Imagine, if Ralph found out about him and George!

His mind drifted back to a trip to New York with George. They had seen *West Side Story* on Broadway.

It the safe darkness of the theatre, he held George's hand as they heard the song: *A Place for Us.*

Someday. Somewhere. But not on Grimalkyn Lane in the year 1963.

CHAPTER 9

The alarm clock sprang to life in Ralph and Katie's bedroom. Ralph woke up with a grunt. But today was Friday and that was a saving grace.

Six AM. Still pitch dark out. This was the start of the darkest time of year.

Katie was beside him, asleep in the nude, as always, like a great beached whale.

"Honey?" he said.

"I don't feel too good. I have a headache," she sighed.

"Again?"

"Yes."

"What about those pills Dr. Robinson gave you?"

"I haven't been taking them. They keep me awake all night."

"Did you tell Dr. Robinson?"

Katie made no reply.

"Well, you have to do something! Seriously, it's your health and you have to take more responsibility. Your blood pressure goes up way high, you could have a heart attack or stroke. And believe me, you don't want that. Now, I want you to call Robinson's office when they open and get an appointment as soon as you can. Katie?"

"I'll do it."

Down the hall, Dickie's clock radio woke him up with strains of *Sugar Shack.* He groaned as he thought of another boring day at T. S. Eliot High. But, wait! It was Friday. He had a date tonight with Dee Dee.

Last week he'd nearly make it to third base. Tonight, he just might score. Slam it out of the park! Life could be beautiful. Sometimes.

Ralph gazed at his image in the mirror as he shaved. He and Katie were back on a more even keel. Plus, the holidays were right around the corner.

Last year's Thanksgiving and Christmas were disasters. Michelle's death was still too recent. This year's might not be so bad, that is, if nobody in his family got under Katie's skin.

Thanksgiving would be at his brother Jimmy's house, which was big enough to accommodate the whole Casey clan. Dear old Dad was long gone, but Ma would be there, plus all seven of his brothers, with wives and kids.

He went down the list in his mind: First and foremost was Ma's favorite, Bishop Joseph Casey. Ma knew from the day he was born that he would be a priest. All the other brothers called him Holy Joe. He was an auxiliary in this archdiocese. Ralph thought of him as the cardinal's top yes-man.

Then Ben Casey, just like the doctor on TV, only he ran a lawn and garden center. Sean Casey Paving. Paul Casey Mortgage. Peter Casey Home Improvement. Jimmy Casey Chevrolet. Liam Casey Plumbing and Heating. Finally, bringing up the caboose of this runaway train, there was Ralph.

Katie was never comfortable at Casey family gatherings. So many boisterous children got on her nerves. But it ran deeper than that.

He never thought his family cared for Katie, nor she for them. For starts, their wedding had been way too expensive. None of his married brothers went through anything like that. Not even the bishop's ordination had been so over the top.

When Dear Old Dad saw Katie, in her bridal splendor, he had whispered, "I must say, Son, you got your money's worth. That's the Giant Economy Size."

But things got worse at their first Thanksgiving together. Katie asked for seconds on turkey, gravy and stuffing. Ma smiled sweetly and said, "You don't need them, Dear."

Only the bishop turned to his mother and said, "Ma!" The rest of the brothers howled with laughter. Katie stayed mad till the following Spring.

Plus, it had been at Ma's insistence that Dickie and Michelle had been baptized as infants. The fact that the children had never been taken back to church lowered the temperature even more, between Ma and Katie. "Worse than Kennedy and Khrushchev," Ralph mumbled.

Did Katie know that Ralph's mother had attended Michelle's memorial? That might make things a lot worse.

Ralph had called Jimmy's wife to make sure that Ma and Katie were seated at the table as far apart as possible. She agreed, that was a wise precaution.

If there was a sunny side to any of this, it was that there would be no contact with Claire during this so-called happiest of all seasons. Katie refused to even consider such a thing. "I have no sister! Not after what she did. I hate her and I don't give a damn what she does!"

"Yeah, right," Ralph said, wiping his face with a towel. "That time of year again. Peace on Earth, and what did Tiny Tim say? God bless us, everyone."

Downstairs, Dickie was shoveling the Breakfast of Champions into his mouth in front of the TV. Kennedy's smiling face was on. He'd be making a speech later today. Maybe that would cheer Katie up.

Ralph told him to turn the TV off. His mother was not feeling well.

"She's sick? Again? What is it now?"

"I don't know. I told her, call the doc, get to the bottom of this. Maybe she needs to go back to the hospital for more tests."

Katie had been in Mercy Hospital, so many times. The tests always yielded the same result. She had to lose at least sixty pounds as a start.

"I've tried," she would always say. "I can't."

The last time Katie was there had been in June. She had some sort of attack. Ralph never had figured out what it was. They had all been at the breakfast table. Ralph handed the *Clarion* to Dickie and said, "Get a load of that!"

There was a Buddhist monk, in a serene prayer pose, totally in flames.

Katie had jumped up from her chair and started fighting for breath. Ralph called an ambulance and shouted, "Make it quick!" Once at Mercy, Katie got a shot to calm her down and one night's stay for observation. Then she was fine. That was damn scary, whatever it was.

Ralph went upstairs to check on Katie before leaving. She had not moved.

"Please don't turn on the light," she said, "it hurts my eyes when I get these headaches."

"You think you'll be all right?"

"Yes."

"You want me to turn the radio on for some classical music?"

"That would be nice."

"Call me at work if you need anything. And for gosh sakes, don't forget to call Robinson's office at nine sharp."

"I'll do it, Ralph. I'll do it."

"'Bye, Honey."

"Good-bye, Ralph." she sighed, as if for the last time.

CHAPTER 10

Katie did not go back to sleep. She rolled over in bed. The springs squeaked. She thought about how much she hated Claire and hoped Claire would be by herself and miserable over the holidays.

This was nothing new between them. Katie and Claire never had gotten along, even before Michelle came to be. Their animosity went back to their parents' miserable marriage.

Katie took after their father, a big man with big healthy appetites. She ended up with his large frame and his weight control problems. Claire was like their mother, small and sprightly, with a dancer's build.

Mother had explained the facts of life to Katie once she was old enough to understand. "For a woman to have sexual relations with a man is a sin. If you just met him in a bar, or married him in church, it's a sin. Even though if you're married, it's a woman's obligation. Men like it. Such pigs. They act like wild animals. We don't. We know better. It's dirty and disgusting and the real reason why Adam and Eve got thrown out of Eden."

"Then why do people bother with it at all?" Katie asked.

"Because it's the only way we can get babies. That's the tragedy of it."

In those days, Katie's father worked in the office of a big shipping company. His co-worker and best friend was Richard Keller. Richard was engaged to Rose O'Toole, the prettiest girl in St. Patrick's parish.

One of Katie's early memories was going with her parents to their wedding. The bride looked like a fairy princess. This started Katie's plans for the wedding of her dreams.

She saw her mother speaking to the bride before the ceremony and thought of Mother saying: *Close your eyes and think of England.*

The marriage was all too short. On their Vermont honeymoon, Richard fell out of a canoe and drowned.

Fear death by water. Who said that?

Rose was alone in the world, a widow with no children but with spectacular Irish beauty. Katie's father was such a comfort to her in her grief. Yes, and more. So much more.

After Claire's birth, Mother got wise to what was going on. She would never consider divorce. "Too disgraceful. And I'll not set that bum free!" But she banned him from their bedroom. There would be no more babies. From then on, Mr. Quinn slept in the spare room, unless he was spending the night with Mrs. Keller. Which was often.

Rarely did her parents speak directly to each other. There was a chance they might reconcile during Claire's illness, but once Claire recovered, Mr. Quinn was back with Mrs. Keller.

"Shameless hussy!" her mother said. "They're the talk of the town but they don't care. No decency at all!"

Katie rolled over again. She thought of the time Claire was so critically sick. Polio, they said it was. A terrible thing; the scourge of the neighborhood in the summer of 1928.

Claire had been crabby and whiny all day and would not eat her dinner. "But Mommy, I don't feel good!" she protested.

Mother took her temperature. She did have a slight fever. Mother put her to bed. At bedtime, she was sound asleep. At midnight, she was awake and crying, "Mommy!"

"Oh, dear, oh dear!" her mother was saying. "Where does it hurt, Baby? Where?"

Naturally, their father was at Mrs. Keller's. Mother wrapped Claire's tiny body in a blanket and told Katie, "I have to get her to the hospital right away. Can I trust you to be a good girl and stay in your bed?"

Katie realized she had no choice in the matter. She crawled under her own covers. "Your father will be back before you wake up in the morning. Like the tom cat he is!"

Katie heard Mother's Model T sputter to life. Then she was alone.

Alone, she recalled, and about to meet the ghosts and the dragon that would haunt her for the rest of her life. Katie trembled to think of it. Best not to do so. Too frightening.

Besides, the radio was playing Gluck's *Dance of the Blessed Spirits.* In the mind she could see them, softly gliding around the ceiling light fixture. How happy it made her to see their dance. It reminded her of the happiest day of her life, when she felt she could fly.

Katie drifted off into a half-sleep, half-awake state. She was strolling in a garden with President Kennedy. He wore his formal outfit from his Inauguration; Katie was naked as she was in real life. Rather like Eve, before she fell.

"You don't mind?" she asked him.

"Darling, I love you just the way you are. Don't lose an ounce." He gave her bulging midriff an affectionate squeeze.

"But Jackie…"

"Never mind Jackie. You are the one I love most."

"Jackie always dresses in such fine style."

"And those bills she's running up are beyond belief!"

"She speaks fluent French. I only know a few words."

They came to the end of the garden path. "I have to leave now, Darling," he said with a small kiss.

"Oh," said Katie. "Au revoir, Jack," she told him.

"Adieu, Katie."

"But, Jack, why do you say that? It means forever."

Jack pressed two fingers on her lips and whispered, Ask not. Then he was gone.

Katie was fully awake with a start. What did Jack mean by that? Has she misunderstood him?

Then the radio went silent. There was some static. Was there some problem? Katie reached for the dial, thinking, bring the *Blessed Spirits* back!

"Ladies and Gentlemen, we interrupt this broadcast to bring you a bulletin. Shots were fired at the president's motorcade in Dallas. At this point, we have no information as to the condition of the president or the first lady. Stay tuned to this station and we will bring you updates as they occur."

Katie rolled out of bed, landed hard on the floor, voided her bladder into the carpet, and howled as if she were being burned at the stake.

"Jack!" she screamed. "Jack, no!"

Math class had to be the most boring ever. Dickie eyed Dee Dee, three rows over. Dee Dee was paying good attention and taking notes. Big deal. Tonight, she was going to prove her love for him, once and for all. Tonight, or it was over.

If Dee Dee won't, Dickie could find someone who will. After all, girls found him irresistible.

Several other boys were looking at Dickie, poking one another, snickering, making obscene gestures, and paying no attention to the equation on the board.

Tony, behind Dickie, nudged the back of his chair and said, "Hey! Teach asked you a question, Knucklehead!"

The whole class giggled. "I had no idea that any of this was so uproariously funny," the teacher said. "Perhaps you might have something to say about this equation, Mr. Casey? Well? Do you care to enlighten us?"

Dickie hemmed and hawed, then a blast of static came over the PA system. "Attention all students and staff," said the principal. "We have received word that President Kennedy was shot on his way into Dallas. He was taken to Parkland Hospital. As yet we have no word as to the extent of his injuries."

A shock wave surged through the classroom. Several girls screamed. Math class was virtually over until the bell rang for the next class. As Dickie made his way to English, the PA came alive again.

"All students and staff," said the principal in a shaking voice. "Reliable sources have confirmed that President Kennedy has died. Classes for the rest of the day are cancelled and suspended till further notice. All students are requested to return directly to their homes in an orderly manner. Teachers, meet me in Prufrock Hall."

Dickie would remember all Hell breaking loose in the corridors. Teachers were trying to restore order. He spotted Dee Dee with a group of girls by the up staircase.

"Oh, Dickie!" she said, her face pallid and wet with tears. "Oh. Dickie, I'm scared, what are we going to do now?"

"Well, um, I was thinking. We don't have to go straight home, do we? I mean, you and me, we could go off someplace and…"

Dee Dee looked at him in horror. Then he felt the sting of her hand across face. She tore off his class ring and threw it at him.

"Snake!" she shouted, and ran down the corridor, sobbing.

Dickie stood for a while with a blank expression, then picked up his ring and slowly meandered in the direction of the exit.

In a downtown office tower, Ralph wondered what the Hell was going on.

"Mr. Casey!" his secretary sobbed. "Somebody shot the president! He's dead!"

"No, he's not," said another secretary. "He's still alive on Channel Two!"

"Dear God, what have I done?" Ralph said to himself. "I left Katie alone, with the radio on. If she hears this and she's all alone, what's going to happen?"

Ralph grabbed his coat, ready to run to Employee Parking. Then he decided, no. Best to call. Maybe Katie had turned off the radio and did not know yet.

"I'll talk to her," he said, dialing his home number. "I'll tell her to leave the radio and TV off. Stay inside. Leave the shades down. Don't answer the doorbell. And don't answer the phone if it rings before I get home. No, Honey, this is not a nuclear war with Russia. Stay put, everything's going to be all right!"

His home phone rang. And rang. Ralph saw it on the night stand, ringing over and over. No one picked up.

Katie was in the living room, in front of the black and white TV, as the news from Dallas turned more ominous. Someone said Jackie was crawling on the back of the limo, reaching for something. Word was, Jack was in Parkland Hospital, that much she knew. Then there was an item, that two Catholic priests were seen walking out of Parkland, looking grim.

Then there was no further denial. "Ladies and Gentlemen," the announcer intoned, "the President of the United States is dead."

Katie shrieked and tore out tufts of her hair, then ran out the front door as if she were on fire. She made it halfway up the block, where she saw Brunhilde circling the Wagners' oak tree and howling. Even animals knew something terrible had happened.

A strange bearded man tried to block her way. Katie threw a punch at him, hard enough to break his nose. He ducked it.

"Mrs. Casey, please!" "You must know me. I'm your neighbor, Dan Doyle. Can you understand me?"

He was holding a large cloth: a child's quilt with an image of Davy Crockett, fighting a bear.

"Jack!" she screamed. "Jack!"

"No, no, Mrs. Casey, I'm not Jack Kennedy, I'm Dan Doyle. I need to help you."

"Then help me find Jack! They took him away!"

"Please. Mrs. Casey. There's something else you need to do first. You ran out of your house with no clothes on."

"How dare you say that! I would never do such a thing!"

Only then did Katie realize she was as naked as the day she was born. Dan wrapped her in the quilt and guided her back home. "See? You even left the front door wide open. You don't want to do that, do you?"

He kept talking to her, trying to quiet her down. "Yes, yes, I know what happened. First my editor called me. Then my attorney. Then my agent. Then my mother! Was I ever surprised to hear from her! She doesn't quite approve of me."

Once inside, Dan sat Katie down on the living room sofa. He had never been in this house before and was somewhat surprised that the furniture was not covered in plastic. The TV was still disgorging the latest news from Dallas. The phone on the kitchen wall kept ringing. Dan was not about to answer the Casey phone.

"We have to get some clothes on you," Dan said. "Can you make it upstairs?"

"I don't think I can. Where did they take Jack? I'm dizzy."

"Then you stay there, and I'll go up and get you something. Don't go near that door, now."

"I think I'm going to throw up."

"Try not to."

Dan passed a closed room, which had at one time been Michelle's. Then the shambles that was Dickie's room. Then he entered the forbidden sanctum, where Ralph and Katie *oh please I don't want to think about what they do in here.*

The curtains were drawn so the room was dark. Dan turned on the overhead light. The bed was like Katie herself: unmade, unkempt. Discarded clothing was all over, and the whole room reeked of urine and sickness. Who would not be depressed in a place like this?

But where to start?

Dan took a quick peek into the nightstand, then slammed it shut. That answered one of his questions. Was Ralph armed? Now he knew.

He pulled open a closet. There was that ugly pink housedress. He pulled open a bureau drawer and found Ralph's boxer shorts. Wrong! The other bureau yielded Katie's ex-large bras and panties. He grabbed a handful of them, threw them on the bed, and took a few downstairs.

Katie was still on the sofa. She asked Dan to turn off the TV, which he did. Whoever was on the phone had hung up.

"Now, look," he explained. "I need you to put these things on a quickly as possible. Because any minute, Ralph is going to walk right through that door."

Ralph, whom I dislike immensely. Ralph, who has a mean streak a mile wide. Ralph, who is armed.

"I need you to think about this. If he finds me, alone, with his wife, in his house, and his wife is naked, what's he going to think?"

"I don't know," Katie sighed.

"Well, I do!"

First, he struggled to get the panties over Katie's thighs, then all the way up. So far, so good. Then he put on her bra and fastened it in back. Finally, he pulled the housedress over her. Not very neat, but it would have to do.

"Mrs. Casey? I don't want to have to leave you now. But I really have no choice. Will you do this for me? Just sit tight here till Ralph gets home."

"Yes, she promised. "Yes, I will."

"Thank you so much," he said, pulled the front door shut on his way out and sighed.

"Yes," she said, "Yes, I'll stay here till Ralph gets home." Dan was reminded of the faithless Molly Bloom's soliloquy from Ulysses.

"Yes. Yes. Yes. Yes, Ralph. Yes, Dan. Yes, Jack, Mr. President, yes, yes, yes. Anything you say, yes."

Dan ran back to his house, locked the door behind him and dialed the phone. He had been on the phone with George when he saw the naked Katie charging down the sidewalk. "George, I have to run now, I'll call you right back!"

George picked up on the first ring. "Hello? Dan?"

"George, thank God."

"Dan? Are you all right?"

"Um, sort of. Look, I was wondering, can you come over for dinner tonight? Please? It's been a difficult day and there's something I need to tell you."

"Sure! Will six be all right?"

"It will be perfect."

"See you then, Hot Stuff."

"Take care."

Dan hung up and doubted this twenty-second day of November 1963, could get any worse. But you never knew, did you? You never knew.

CHAPTER 11

Dickie decided to walk home. The school bus was full of weeping girls. Even though he had enough change in his pocket, he didn't want the rapid transit bus, either. No doubt about it, that bus, too, would be full of tearful girls When girls cried, they gave him the willies.

He stopped off at the drugstore, to check the latest centerfolds on the magazine rack. The manager chased him out.

"Kid, don't you know that the president's dead? This place is closing. Every place else is already closed. Go on home to Mommy and Daddy."

Dickie walked through the park, sat on a bench, and pulled his class ring from his pocket. It had been filled with a blob of wax so it would fit Dee Dee's smaller finger. He pulled the wax out and squashed it beneath his shoe.

"My baby done left me, my baby done gone," he lamented. "I'm singing the blues, 'cause she done me wrong."

What a song that would make, if he knew how to write it. Elvis would record it. He'd get rich.

Dickie managed to get home as dusk fell. The were no cars in the driveway. He let himself in through the kitchen door. No lights were on.

"Mom? Dad?"

No answer. That was odd.

He looked upstairs. His room was the same. As for his parents' room, it looked like somebody set off a bomb in it. Bureau drawers were hanging open. His mother's clothing and underwear was tossed about.

"Mom? Where's everybody go?"

Again, his words bounced off the walls.

Since Dickie did not know what to do, he went downstairs, raided the fridge, and turned on the TV. Then he sat on the sofa to await further instruction.

Further instruction came soon enough, in the form of Ralph, bursting through the front door and cursing the traffic. "Where's your mother?" he demanded.

"Gee, Dad, I don't know. I kind of just got here myself."

"Dickie, where is she?" The he bellowed, "Katie! Katie, I'm home! Katie?"

No answer.

"Dad…" Dickie was about to explain that there was a mess in the master bedroom. Ralph bounded up the stairs too fast, then shouted, "Dickie!"

"Yeah?"

"Did you see what went on in here?"

"I didn't do it, Dad."

"I'm not saying you did! I said, did you see who did do it?"

"Um, no."

"And where is your mother?"

"I don't know."

"How can you not know?"

"She must be around here. Isn't her car in the garage where she left it?"

"Dickie!" Ralph thundered, "there is no car in that garage at all! Katie! Where are you?"

Silence.

"Oh, my God, Dickie. Oh, my God. You know she's not well. And how she feels about Kennedy. If she was alone when she heard he's dead, there's no saying what she will try."

"What can we do about it?"

"I'll show you," Ralph said. "See this flashlight?"

"Um, yeah."

Ralph turned it on. "You are going to do a complete search of the house and yard, including the garage, shed and your idiotic treehouse. Then, the attic. Go find your mother and bring her back here."

Ralph sat on the sofa as Dickie blundered about. He thought of the last time he pulled down the attic stairs. He had been passing boxes of Michelle's belongings to Avocet at the top of the stairs.

Since Avocet and Michelle were the same size, in a rare spasm of generosity, Ralph told Avocet to take some of Michelle's clothing and her good winter coat. "But whatever you do," Ralph cautioned her, "don't wear any of that stuff here, where Mrs. Casey can see it. No telling what she'll do."

Avocet agreed. She could not admit to Ralph, that she was too uncomfortable with the idea if her wearing a dead person's clothing, no matter how nice it was. As soon as she could, she took all of it to Goodwill.

Michelle's guitar went up there too. Somehow it got so badly broken, there was no point in trying to sell it.

Dickie did as he was told. The attic creeped him out, with its cobwebbed remains of his sister's short life. But there was no Katie to be found.

"Katie, Katie, Katie!" Ralph called out. "Can you hear me?"

"Dad? Do you think we'd better call the cops?"

"Absolutely not. No cops! And I'll tell you why. I can't deal with them anymore. Not after what your sister put us through. Those same questions they asked me, over and over again, trying to trap me, to see if I'd change my story. To see if I'd confess to something I didn't do. I'm not going through that, ever again."

Dickie was amazed. Dad had said, your sister, meaning Michelle.

"No. Here is what we are going to do. Katie could not have gone far. So, we are going to go out in my car and find her."

"But where are we going to look?"

"Where does she go when she leaves this house?"

"Food Fair," said Dickie, "and that's about it. Only Food Fair's closed because…"

"Yes, yes, I know."

"Maybe she went to St. Agatha's to pray?"

Ralph nodded. "That would be a first, but we need to check it out. Can you think of any place else?"

"Claire's house?" Dickie asked.

"She hates Claire."

"Yeah, but Claire's her closest relative, so maybe she went there."

"I think you might have good idea," Ralph replied.

"Dad? Wouldn't it be easier to call Claire first? She's in the book, isn't she?"

"No, I think it would be better if we went over there. Surprise her. Maybe shake her up a little so if she knows anything, she won't hold out on us. Claire's going to learn that she's not dealing with a couple of fools!"

CHAPTER 12

George's car turned into Dan's driveway just after Ralph and Dickie took off.

"Thank God you're here," Dan welcomed him.

"I got us some wine to go with dinner."

"Good, because we're going to need it." Once the door was closed, they exchanged a brief kiss. Dan told George to sit down, the steaks were just about done.

"Oh. How's Moby Dickie?" George asked.

"He was about to wreck an oil tanker, when I got the first of many calls."

"And the gallant Charlie Ahab?"

"Still hasn't got a clue."

George regarded Lyndon Johnson on the TV screen. "Is he still the vice president?"

"Nope," said Dan, "he was sworn in on Air Force One."

"Did he say yee-haw?"

"Would not surprise me. Anyhow, he's our president now. Jackie was a witness."

"God love her! And she still has to explain it to the little ones. Just not right. Did they say who did it yet?"

"They've got some creep in custody by the name of Lee Harvey Oswald."

"Is that him on the screen now? Looks like he's not up to anything good."

"That's him. Only we don't know yet, what he did. Seems he killed a cop. But, Kennedy? We just don't know and he's not saying. He gets a fair trial like everybody else. Sit down and let's dig in, and I'll tell you about the rest of my stranger than fiction day."

"Best idea yet. Believe it or not, I'm starved!"

"How can you think of food at a time like this?"

"How can I not?"

George's eyes grew wide as Dan recounted his story. "I heard a woman screaming, and I looked out the window. There was Katie, running toward Frieda Wagner's fence, every bit as naked as a jaybird."

"Katie Casey? The big lady across the street?"

"The very one. Married to Ralph, who keeps giving me dirty looks. She rarely goes out, which is why this was such a shock."

"Stark naked?"

"Rubensesque beyond belief. But not something you'd want to see. And she was screaming about Kennedy. I'd heard stories. You know, I'm friends with her sister Claire."

"Oh, yeah, I remember Claire. She's cool."

"Katie hates Claire's guts, but that's beside the point. Anyhow, Claire told me she thinks Katie was obsessed with Jack Kennedy. Wow, is she ever! She was totally flipped out, and when I tried to help her she threw a punch at me."

"You ducked, I presume?"

"You presume correctly. I was able to get through to her and convince her that she didn't have anything on. And I covered her with that quilt over there, which I've had for a while."

"Davy, Davy Crockett," George sang, "King of the Wild Frontier."

"Wait, it gets wilder. Okay. I got her back to her living room."

"Is it really like you thought it was? Everything covered in plastic?"

"No! Not Early Pat Nixon at all. More like Late Ralph Cheapskate. I was getting scared. Here she was, naked and not well. But what scared me more was the idea that Ralph might walk in any minute."

"And find you like that with his wife. I'd say you had a problem."

"She couldn't get up the stairs. I had to run up to their bedroom."

"Oh, no!"

"I had to work fast. That means, I had to get her underthings out of her bureau. I just tossed them on the bed and picked out a few. And a dress. And I took them down and got her dressed as best I could. I made her promise me she'd wait there for Ralph. And I left. Quickly."

"You ransacked Ralph and Katie's bedroom. I can't believe this."

"I wish it had never happened. Oh, one other thing. When I was looking around, I opened up the nightstand drawer. There's a gun in it."

"Oh, great! Was it loaded?"

"Do you think I'm going to pick it up and find out?"

"Wise decision on your part, Dan. You know, I would have done the same thing."

"I don't know, George. I keep asking myself, did I do the right thing? Should I have called an ambulance for Katie, or something?"

"You want my honest opinion?"

"No, I want Dear Abby's. Yes, I want yours!"

"What you did was right, Dan. You got her off the street, quieted down, and dressed. And you took a big risk doing it. Suppose you called an ambulance, the cops, whatever? You'd have to deal with this Ralph down the line. And from what you've told me of Ralph, gratitude is not what he'd be feeling. He'd say you stuck your nose in his family's business. You were in his house, his bedroom even. He'd have a fit."

"Plus, he's armed."

"That, too. No, I think you deserve a medal for what you did today. Not that you will ever get one."

"I just hope she stayed put like I said."

"Where would she go? She'll be all right."

They put the dishes in the sink and went into the family room, where NBC News was still on TV with the volume low. "Too depressing," they decided. Dan turned on his record player and took an album from the top of his stack of Broadway hits. It happened to be *Camelot.* They sat on the sofa, together with their wine.

"You know what?" Dan asked.

"What?"

"I'm so glad this day is over."

"As am I. But there's always tomorrow."

"Sufficient for the day is the evil thereof. Let's not think about it, Hon."

They started in on a long kiss, and became tangled on the sofa. Then the phone on the end table sprang to life.

"If that's my mother again," Dan sighed.

"What will you do?" George asked.

"Go insane."

Dan reached out of the tangle, picked it up and said, "Hello?"

"Dan? I hate to bother you at a time like this. It's Claire."

"Oh, Claire!"

"That's Claire?" said George. "Tell her I said hello!"

"That's George, my half-brother from Peoria. You remember him? He's staying here till things quiet down. He says hello!"

"Hi, George!" she said. "But, look, Dan, I wouldn't call now if I didn't have a problem."

"What's the problem?"

"Ralph."

"Oh, no. What did he do now?"

"He was just here, with Dickie. He was banging so hard on the door. I got scared so I put on the chain lock before I opened the door. And there he was. And he asked me if I knew where Katie had gone."

"Wait. Katie's gone?"

"That's what they said. He can't find her anywhere at home, her car's gone too. And he wanted to know if she was with me. This is the last place she'd be!"

"Ooops," Dan said.

"I told them the truth. Katie did not come over here. Neither had she called me. But they wouldn't believe me, Dan! They insisted on coming in and looking for her. You know how Ralph gets when he mad. I did not let him in. I said, 'Do you have a warrant? Then you're way out of line, Ralph. You'd better go. And if you don't go, I'm calling the police. I mean it.'"

"Did he leave?"

"He gave me such an evil look, Dan. So did Dickie. I was afraid Dickie was going to pull a switchblade on me. He told me I have not heard the last of this. Then they got into Ralph's car and drove away. Please tell me, Dan, have you seen Katie at all?"

"Oh, my Lord," Dan said. "Claire, we need to talk. There's a lot I need to tell you. But I don't feel right, saying it all over the phone. Maybe…maybe you need to come over here. With Ralph behaving like that, I don't want you to be alone tonight."

"I couldn't impose on you."

"I have the guest room all ready."

"But you already have a guest!"

"Oh, yeah, I guess I do. We'll figure something out, don't worry. Here's what I want you to do. Pack a bag. But don't walk out to your car. You don't know what's in the bushes. I'll come over in the Porsche and pick up you up. I'll ring your doorbell three times in a row so you will know it's me. Got it?"

"Got it. I hate to be so much trouble."

"You're not. Go pack and be ready."

He hung up and got his coat and keys.

"Aw, Hon!" said George.

"I shouldn't have left Katie alone. Now Ralph's going after Claire. You hold down the fort. I'll be right back."

"You ought to get another medal," George said. All the other houses on the block were lit up, except for the Casey house, in total darkness. George watched the tail lights of the Porsche vanish into the night.

CHAPTER 13

Somewhere in West Virginia, there was a sputtering neon sign by the highway that said, COZY COVE MOTEL. VACANCY.

Katie pulled into the parking lot, went into the office and took a room for the night. The TV was on in the clerk's office, and on it was a face. A face that went with the name she had heard earlier that day, on her car radio.

Lee Harvey Oswald.

Katie was shaken at how much Oswald resembled Dickie. There was that same wise guy grin Dickie used, when he denied any knowledge of who was blowing up mailboxes. Guilty as sin, is what it said.

Her room was the sort of place that she considered beneath her. It was gross and disgusting by her standards. The shag carpet was stained. The radiator made funny noises. But it would have to suffice for now. She would be dead, so very soon, and this place did not really matter.

Jack came to me. He did not say au revoir. He said Adieu. Forever.

After Dan had dressed her and left her on the sofa, it suddenly dawned on her, what she had to do. She had to be with her beloved Jack Kennedy. Wherever he had gone, she had to go. But there was one task left in her life. It had to be completed first.

Katie would take down that son of a bitch who did this to Jack, Lee Harvey Oswald. Then she would dic in a hail of bullets. Or take her own life. One or the other. Either way, she would be dead soon, and the whole world would know her, and sing her praises forever.

Katie had gone up to her bedroom, which she wrecked even more, hastily packing her suitcase. Then she placed Ralph's handgun in her purse and took cash from the box in the den. Although she knew nothing about how a handgun worked, Ralph often warned her that he kept all six chambers loaded. And that the safety, whatever it was, was off.

It should be easy, then. All she had to do was pull the trigger *and welcome to Hell, Lee Harvey Oswald!* Only she would not grant him a merciful death. First, she'd shoot him in the gut a few times. Make him scream and suffer for what he did.

In her haste to leave the house before Ralph got back, she had not left any sort of note. What could she say? "Ralph, I'm going to Dallas, don't follow me?" Well, never mind. Her family would find out soon enough. Ralph, Dickie, and even Claire were going to be amazed.

They may mourn her and miss her. But some day they would understand, this had to be done, and only Katie Casey had the strength to do it.

But since driving away from home, Katie had been running on pure adrenalin. It could not last. Besides, going through these mountain passes, the November darkness was deep and perilous.

Here be dragons.

The ghosts who had so frightened her as a child? They could well be in those shadows. It was said that here, they lurked in the woods. One could jump out from behind a tree and scare her so much she'd drive off the mountain.

Katie decided to stop for the rest of the night and resume her journey at dawn. She could not let anything keep her from her destiny.

The reception on the little TV in this room was terrible. Still, there was that mocking face. Lee Harvey Oswald.

What power there was, in her white-hot hate. The loathing she felt for Claire was nothing, compared to what she felt for Oswald.

Lee Harvey Oswald, who had murdered John F. Kennedy, who was her protector.

Claire, always Claire! The sickly little sap who took up too much of her mother's attention. It was Claire who made her mother leave her alone. That lead to her encounter with the ghosts.

Speaking of which, Katie bolted the door shut, and pushed the bureau in front of it, in case any ghosts were out there. One could not be too careful.

Katie switched off the TV and the lights. She got into bed and felt the scratchy sheets on her skin. It came back to her, how she came to know that ghosts were real.

Her mother had run off in the night to get Claire to the hospital. Her father was supposed to be back in the morning. He wasn't. Only later did Katie learn that he'd gone out of town with Mrs. Keller.

Katie woke up the following morning to an empty house. There was plenty of food in the kitchen: cereal, oranges, Uneeda biscuits and milk. She knew she was not supposed to answer the door when she was alone. Mother said there were bad people out there. If an adult opened the door, they would try to discuss business. But if a little girl did, they would club her over the head and chop her up for an Irish stew. No one rang the doorbell all day.

She spent the day reading her books and listening to the radio. Still, no word from anyone. What was wrong with Claire, did she die?

By dinner time, her supply of Uneeda biscuits was starting to run low. Perhaps she ought to venture out and find a responsible grown-up. First, she went to a place she was not supposed to go. That was Mrs. Keller's house. But there was no answer to her knock and her father's roadster was nowhere around.

Katie was getting worried now. Should she ask one of the neighbors for help? Or go to St. Patrick's, which was right around the corner? That might be the better choice. Maybe one of the nuns could help her.

However, no one seemed to be around. No one asked her why a little girl was here all by herself. There was a rack of red vigil lights burning but no other source of light.

Dusk was falling when Katie wandered out to the athletic field behind St. Patrick's. Few people were walking on the street and there were even fewer cars. Katie was starting to get seriously frightened.

"Mommy?" she asked. The sky was growing dark.

There came the sudden sound of many sputtering cars approaching the field, along with a strong odor of gasoline. Katie, terrified, jumped behind the score board. Then the cars parked next to the field and ghosts came out.

Yes, ghosts. Real live ghosts, all in white with dead holes in their faces where eyes were supposed to be. Katie was certain of what she saw. She wet her pants but in her terror, she could not move.

No! No! I must not think of this! Katie hid herself under the worn covers of this bed.

After a while there was perhaps a brief sleep and dream. Katie saw her funeral in the cathedral downtown. The cardinal himself presided, assisted by her brother-in-law Bishop Casey. The place was so packed, crowds spilled into the streets. All three networks carried it on live TV.

In the front pew, Ralph blubbered. Dickie looked lost and frightened. But Claire wept the most of all, because she realized that her life added up to nothing. She would be remembered only as Katie's sister. The sickly one, who never amounted to anything.

CHAPTER 14

Claire did not go near the door till she heard the bell ring three times. There, thank God, was Dan.

"Let's go," he said. "Got everything?"

"You bet. Geez, I hate doing this to you. And George."

"Quit apologizing."

They made their way by Claire's shrubbery, half-expecting Dickie to jump out of it. Then, into the Porsche. *Va-room*!

"All right," said Dan. "When you called earlier, you asked me if I'd seen Katie. The answer is yes. I saw a lot more of Katie than anyone should have to see."

"How do you mean?"

Dan explained how he had seen Katie running down the street in her birthday suit. How he had covered her and taken her home.

"She couldn't even get upstairs, so I had to go get her some clothes and underwear. Fast, too, I was so scared Ralph was about to find me alone in there with her. I made a big mess of their bedroom. Anyhow, I got her dressed, told her to stay put till Ralph got home, and left. And that was the end of it. That's what I thought. Now you say, Katie's missing?"

"That's what Ralph said to me. He can't find her anywhere."

"Hmmm. Oh, one other thing about Ralph."

"What?"

"Did you know he has gun?"

Claire paused and said, "No. I did not know that."

"I totally ripped up their bedroom, looking for Katie's things. I opened the drawer in the nightstand and there it was."

"Loaded?"

"I don't know, I was afraid to touch it."

"I would have felt the same way. Besides, you don't want your prints on it."

"For all I know, maybe it was a toy."

"And for what I know about Ralph and his temper, he would not keep a toy gun in the night stand. No, it would be a real one. You break into his house, and he will blow your head off."

"I guess that almost meant me."

"I just can't believe this. Katie was crazy for Jack Kennedy. But for her to vanish at a time like this? It makes no sense."

"Maybe she's not gone."

"How do you mean?"

"Ralph's so impulsive. Could be she just went out some place, and when Ralph gets home, he'll find her waiting for him."

"I can't imagine where she would go. She was too hoity-toity to be close to any of the neighbors."

"St. Agatha's?"

"I don't think she's ever set foot in there. But I think you're right, this is most likely nothing and Ralph is overreacting the way he always does. And you know Dickie: the wooden dummy on Ralph's knee."

"We're all under a lot of stress."

"We sure are. And Ralph never did handle stress well."

"If you don't mind my saying so, the way he acted when Michelle died, it was horrible. Just horrible. Spreading these lies, that she drowned in the tub. He's said it so often I think he believes it himself."

"Oh, sure he does, because he can't deal with the truth. And Katie, screaming at me, because I wanted Michelle to be remembered like a precious child, not like a failed object to be thrown away and forgotten. But what do I know? Who was I but the Crazy Aunt, Divorced Bad Influence?"

Claire wiped away a tear.

"You loved her," Dan said. "Michelle needed that."

"Thanks," Claire sniffled.

The Porsche arrived at home. George greeted them at the door. The Casey house was still dark.

Somewhere in the night, Ralph and Dickie still prowled. They had disrupted the rosary service at St. Agatha's. No Katie. They even checked around the barren Food Fair parking lot. No Katie.

How strange was this night, like no other! The streets were virtually abandoned. All the stores were shut tight, even the big downtown Bloomberry's, with black-draped pictures of Kennedy in their display windows. There were a few drunks and junkies wandering about. There was a lunatic preacher, shouting to no one, that this was the start of end of the world.

At Jimmy Casey Chevrolet, the showroom window was full of black crepe. The shamrocks and dancing leprechauns were gone.

It occurred to Dickie, what adults had been yelling at him all day was true.

The President's dead.

This had never happened to him before. He began thinking, *this is how Dee Dee felt. I'm scared.*

At one stop they saw a car of the same make, model and year as Katie's. But the plate number was different. Still no Katie.

After midnight, they returned home. It was too dark, Ralph decided, and they were growing weary. They'd figure out their new plan in the morning.

Dickie still thought that they ought to call the cops and report Katie as a missing person. After all, this morning she had been sick again. This morning. It felt like a thousand years ago. But, no. He knew how Ralph felt about it.

No sense in picking an argument. Not with his father. Certainly not now.

CHAPTER 15

To the amazement of many, the sun rose the following morning. Shortly thereafter, Katie checked out of the Cozy Cove and was back on the road heading south and west.

So far, so good. She had half-expected Ralph to raid her room in the night, and plead with her to come back home.

But driving her own car might be a problem, might make her easier to find, just in case Ralph did turn to the police for help. She remembered a film she saw a few years ago, with Dickie and *she whose name must not be spoken.* The kids had asked her to take them to a scary movie.

What was the name of the film? *Sicko?* Katie could not recall. Janet Leigh was the star. She was a secretary who had just stolen $40,000 in cash from one of her boss's clients. And what did she do, to erase her path?

She got rid of her car and traded it in on something else.

Katie had wanted a new car for a while. This one ran well, but was getting a bit shabby. "Surely your brother Jimmy can get you a good deal?" she asked, but Ralph kept on putting it off.

"Wait till August, when Jimmy has to get rid of his '63 models," Ralph said. Then, "Wait and we'll get you a '64 model." Then, wait, wait, wait. That was Ralph for you, Mr. Cheap.

Though she never wanted to get anything used, she had no choice. Once over the line in Kentucky she saw a sign that said:

BLUE GRASS MOTORS

WE BUY-USED-CARS-WE SELL

Ralph had warned her many times that no woman should go into such a place alone. "They will do nothing but take advantage of you," he said, but Janet Leigh seems to have done all right.

Shortly thereafter, Katie left in a late '50s behemoth with fins. The one salesman on duty regarded her trade-in, and looked like the cat who swallowed the canary.

She turned the radio dial in search of an all-news station. None were within range. All she got was a local rendition of *The Wabash Cannonball.*

Katie joined the traffic on the main highway. *Psycho!* That was the name of the film. Poor Janet Leigh; she had been stabbed to death in the shower. Dickie thought it was neat that the film showed all the plumbing fixtures in the bathroom. Katie felt that was vulgar and uncalled-for, and let her son know.

On the street Katie left, the day dawned cold and clear. An exhausted Claire was still sound asleep in Dan's guest room. George insisted he'd spend the night on the Castro Convertible sofa, which Dan had named Fidel. Once Claire had retired, he and Dan folded Fidel out, messed up the sheets, and then vanished into Dan's bedroom.

Before they both fell into a fitful sleep, George said to Dan: "There's a lot going on here I don't understand."

"You and me both," Dan told him.

"No, really. Let's say I'm Ralph."

"I'm so glad you're not."

"Seriously. I'm Ralph. And you're Katie. And one day you just vanish into thin air. No call, no note, no nothing. I'd be so worried about you. I'd go right to the cops and report you as missing. So why won't Ralph do that, do you think?"

"Ralph is his own John Wayne. The rugged individual. Thinks he can save the wagon train by himself. Shoots all the Indians before the cavalry gets there. Never mind that he makes all the problems worse with his bungling. Besides, Ralph doesn't trust cops."

"How so?"

"You remember that business with the mailboxes?"

"It was Dickie who blew them up, right?"

"Damn right. And I think that's another reason Ralph can't stand me: he knows I was the one who called the cops. Yes, I did, even though he has no proof of who called. He feels the cops were way too harsh with his precious darling Dickie. And he still maintains that Dickie was innocent. He even lied and said that Dickie was tucked into his own little beddy-bye that night. Come on, I know what I saw."

"Does he still say that Dickie's going to get a seat in the Senate?"

"Dickie will be lucky if he gets a seat in a prison toilet. But Dickie's his favorite and can do no wrong."

"So, Ralph won't go to the cops no matter what."

"There might be more to it. Something to do with Michelle. Claire knows more about it. We can ask her in the morning."

They fell into a fitful sleep. Dan had a nightmare that he was John Wayne, trying to stop a stampeding herd of cattle, only all the cows were naked Katies. George was stalked through a maze by Lee Harvey Oswald, blasting away and shouting that his new mission was to kill off all queers.

CHAPTER 16

Claire slept till after dawn, half-remembering a scene from long ago. She had come home from the hospital, but was in a wheel chair in the parlor, combing her doll's curly blonde hair. Her mother was upset about something, and had called her own mother over to discuss this urgent matter. Katie had been on the settee, reading a book about how Raggedy Ann saved the family pooch from the dogcatcher.

"Aw! Sweetums!" Grandma said, heading right for Claire. "Feeling any better today?"

"I'm not sick any more, Grandma," Claire said. "But I can't walk without my crutches and braces. And I have to go to the crippled children's place and do all these exercises and sometimes they hurt really bad."

"My baby angel," said Grandma, giving Claire a big hug. "What's your dolly's name?"

"She's my Baby Jane doll," said Claire. "She used to be Katie's but Katie gave her to me."

Katie shot her a look that said, *Like Hell I did. Mommy forced me.*

"I'll tell you one thing," said Grandma. "If you stick with your exercises, even if they hurt, some day you will be able to walk and run like other little girls! Wouldn't you like that?"

"No, Grandma. I want to dance like Baby Jane."

"Aw, my brave little sweetie! You will, I just know it!"

Grandma briefly greeted Katie and asked how the new school year was going.

"It's all right," Katie muttered, thinking *I have Sister Mary Lawrence for third grade. I hate her. I am going to make her miserable.*

"Katie still won't say much. Not here, not in school. I don't know why; Lord knows, I've tried everything," Mother explained. "That's the most she's said in ages."

Grandma retreated to the kitchen where Mother had tea ready. "All right, tell me as slowly as you can, what happened. My hearing is not what it used to be."

"I took him back. You knew that. With Claire being so sick, and Katie having problems of her own, plus that disturbance."

"Yes, I heard about that disturbance."

"I felt I could not make it on my own any more. He came back. Moved in to the spare room. Promised to behave himself. Or so I thought!"

"What did he do?"

Mother squeezed a lemon into her tea. How bitter it must have tasted.

"My friend Edna called. She'd been to the Greenhouse Café. And sure enough, there were the two of them. Him and Mrs. Keller. Seated at a table for two. Gazing into each other's eyes. Whispering sweet nothings. He reached over, picked up her hand, and kissed it. As if it were the holy relic of a saint. Edna saw the whole thing."

"Oh, dear."

"My mind is made up. He can stay here as long as he wants, provided he pays the bills. Including all of Claire's medical expenses. But I have nothing to say to that lowlife. And he knows why."

They were interrupted by a blood-curdling shriek from the parlor.

Katie had crept up behind Claire's wheel chair and repeated in a high-pitched mocking voice, "And I have to go to the crippled children's place and do all these exercises and sometimes they hurt really bad. This is going to hurt a lot worse!" Katie grasped both of Claire's pigtails and pulled as hard as she could. Claire dropped Baby Jane. Katie tossed the doll out of her sister's reach. Baby Jane landed on the sofa in a compromising position, with both legs thrust into the air.

"My poor darling!" Grandma said, picking up Claire.

Mother landed on Katie. "Bad girl!" she shouted. "Bad, bad girl to do such a hateful thing to your sick little sister." Then she turned Katie over her knee, pulled her dress up, her panties down, gave her a good hard spanking, and exiled her to her room. "No supper for you tonight, Young Lady. You need to think about what you did."

Many years later, Claire woke up wondering where she was. *This is Dan's house, she recalled, the president's dead. I'm here because Katie ran away. Again.*

George was the first to wake up. "Hon?" he asked Dan.

"Hmmmm?"

"All right if your half-brother from Peoria takes a little walk?"

"That's a great idea. Tell him I said so."

Across the street, Ralph, awake, poured himself a cup of coffee. He had to think.

Perhaps Katie had checked herself into a hospital. He had called Mercy, Beth Israel, all the other local ones. None had a patient named Katie Casey. Scratch that.

Then he decided to take an inventory, not of what was there, but of what was not. Katie's winter coat and purse were gone. So was her suitcase, and several hundred dollars that had been in a box in the den. There were empty hangers in her closet where her housedresses had been. As for her underwear, he had no clue as to what she took.

But what about those pills Dr. Robinson had prescribed for her? She had to have them. The pill bottle was still in the medicine cabinet.

"Oh, my dear Lord, what's she gone and done?"

Dickie was still sound asleep. Ralph needed more coffee. He turned on the TV.

Today, Saturday, there would be a private wake at the White House. Charles DeGaulle had announced he would attend the funeral. As would Prince Philip. The list of foreign dignitaries heading for Washington grew longer by the minute.

"They will bring the whole world with them." Ralph took another gulp. Suddenly he spat out a mouthful of coffee on the kitchen table.

"That's it! Katie went to Washington for the funeral! Dickie? Dickie!"

He ran upstairs and began to stuff his own suitcase. "Ye-ah?" his sleepy-eyed son asked.

"Pack your things. We're going to Washington."

"What for?"

"For the president's funeral, you dope!"

"Why? Did Jackie invite us?"

"No! Because that's where your mother went!"

"Did Mom tell you so?"

"Don't you see? That's the only explanation that makes any sense."

"Dad?"

"Yes?"

"Won't there be a lot of people there? I mean, how are we going to find her?"

"We'll figure that out once we get there. But we can't do anything from here. Take enough stuff for a few days, load it in the trunk, and let's go."

Dickie scratched his head and muttered, "I guess you're right. Hope this works."

Ralph packed just about everything in his bureau. Did he know anyone in or near Washington who could put him and Dickie up? Well, no. As for getting a hotel room, at this point, forget it!

What was he going to do? Move in with Charles DeGaulle? Probably not.

He'd figure something out. Meanwhile, it occurred to him, there was one other thing he was going to need.

What would it be like out on the highway? Or in Washington? Would there be a breakdown of law and order? Riots? Civil disorder? Looting? Who knew!

He reached into the night stand and his hand closed on nothing.

"Dickie!" he thundered. No answer. "Dickie!"

He found his son in the driveway, loading suitcases into the trunk while talking to Frieda Wagner. She'd been walking Brunhilde.

"Yeah?"

"Get over here!"

"You don't have to get sore or nothing. I said I'd go with you."

"Get over here right now. How in the Goddam Hell many times have I told you? You do not, under any circumstances whatsoever, touch my gun!"

Frieda's eyes grew wide, and Brunhilde's ears twitched.

"I didn't touch it, Dad!"

"Then how come it's not in the night stand drawer? Where it belongs?"

"Gee, I don't know."

"Gee, you don't know a damn thing, do you?"

Dickie said nothing.

"If not you, then who? Wo else has been up there?"

"Just Mom."

"That's ridiculous. You know your mother has no experience with firearms. And she knows as well as you do, it's loaded. No, that's stupid. Dammit, the one time I need it, it's gone. Let's make sure we have everything else we need. And let's get the Hell out of here. You know, your mother forgot to take her pills? Here! You hold her pill bottle! We can't waste any more time."

CHAPTER 17

Dan and Claire were in the family room with the TV on when George came back.

"You had a good long walk," Dan told him.

"We were getting worried about you," Claire added.

"Oh, my Lord," said George. "You will not believe what just happened."

"I don't believe any of this," Dan replied, gesturing at the TV. "But try me."

"I'm so bad with names. I forgot already. Who is that nice German lady with the dachshund?"

"Frieda Wagner. And Brunhilde. Why?"

"She saw the whole thing. And she told me."

"Told you what? Take a deep breath and sit down."

"OK. Katie's still missing."

"Overnight?" said Claire. "Not good."

"Ralph had this idea, that she went to Washington for the funeral. He and Dickie packed up the car and went after her."

"How could Ralph, in all his brilliance assume a thing like that?" Claire asked.

"Well, he did. And another thing. He wanted to take his gun with him, only that's gone, too."

"It sure as Hell was there Friday," said Dan, "when I opened the drawer."

"But it's gone now," George replied.

"When Ralph gets an idea in his mind, not even a stick of dynamite in his ear will get it out," Claire told them. "But, no. There's something totally off here. Katie did not go the president's funeral. That does not sound like the Katie I grew up with."

"How do you figure that?"

"Katie doesn't like dead people. Well, not really. And I'm sure she still loves Jack Kennedy, dead or alive. It's just that funerals and wakes and dead people have always bothered her. As kids, we weren't allowed to go. But then we were, when our grandparents died, after we became teens. Katie went to only one: Grandmother Quinn's. She complained it creeped her out to see Grandmother Q in an open casket wearing a ton of makeup. When our other grandparents died, she flat-out refused to go. Mother got mad. Said it was disrespectful. But Katie wouldn't budge. That's just her way, she'd try anything to wiggle out of going to a funeral."

"Ralph does not seem to be aware of that," Dan said.

"I don't know why. His family is huge. His mother had eight babies, all boys, all of whom are wildly successful. (Except for you-know-who.) In a big Irish Catholic family like that, some relative is always dying. There's a raucous wake and long funeral Mass. And Katie never goes, always has an excuse. She's sick. Or having another blow-up with Ma Casey. If it's not one excuse, it's another. When you die, it's a safe bet that Katie Casey is going to be a no-show."

Claire sighed. "Which sounds pretty bad, I know. And I'm hard on Katie a lot. It wasn't easy, growing up with her as my big sister. And I'm sure it's hard on Ralph, being married to her. But there are times I've asked myself, perhaps something bad happened to her when she was a kid. Something I don't know about."

"What makes you think so?" Dan asked.

"For instance, when I had polio I was in the hospital for a long time. And when I got home, Katie wasn't speaking. To anyone! I thought she was jealous of me for getting all the attention. But this wasn't like she was mad. More like she could not speak because she was too scared. Of something that was done to her."

"No one ever said, of what?"

"All our mother would say is that we don't talk about it. That was her way. Whatever it is, bury it."

"And your father?"

"He was rarely around. The fact is, they were so miserable together, he had a mistress. Actually, a parade of mistresses."

"Wow, all at once?"

"Mercy, no! He had the decency to keep it down to one at a time. I do remember the first one, Rose Keller, his best friend's widow. She was the prettiest by far of the lot. Dad lived with us while he carried on with her, but after she died, Mother tossed him out of our house because he took Rose's death so hard. He moved into an apartment. Mom and Dad were never legally divorced."

"What did this Rose die of?" George asked. "As the Wicked Witch of the West said, a little poison?"

"No, and after so long it's all fuzzy. I guess I was about eight. But she had a bad fall, hit her head, and died within a year. Their affair was a big secret, which the whole world knew.

Most of Dad's time was spent with Rose. Still, I owe Katie for some inspiration. She started me on my life path."

"How did she manage to do that?"

"I wanted to cure her, by giving her back her voice. That's why I became a speech therapist, to give lost voices back. Only Katie didn't need my cure. After a while her words came back. As I recall, the first ones were nasty."

"But we still don't know where she is now," Dan offered.

"And we have a gun missing too," George added.

Claire added, "And we don't know where the gun went, either. I don't think it grew legs and walked away on its own."

"George and I had this discussion last night after you went to bed. It seems the most rational thing Ralph could do, is report Katie to the cops as a missing person."

"Did I just hear you use the words Ralph and rational in the same sentence?" Claire asked.

"Ooops, but I was telling George, Ralph has a problem with the cops. Ever since Dickie got caught blowing mailboxes up."

"I know, I know," said Claire. "Plus, according to Ralph, Dickie was as innocent as a newborn lamb. Of course, he is! But there's more to Ralph's history with the cops. Much more. It's hard to say this. And it will be hard for you guys to hear it. But you need to, if you want to understand why Ralph is acting like this. And why Katie is in so much danger."

Claire took a deep breath.

"It goes back to Michelle. As you know, she was forced to drop out of St. Ethel's. Katie was upset. But Ralph was livid. At Michelle, not at those rich bitches who had been tormenting her. She had a chance to push the whole family way up the social ladder. And she blew it.

"What's more, the headmistress was sending her home with a referral to a psychiatrist for her depression. Which Katie regarded as a great disgrace, and Ralph would never allow. Remember, in our family we don't talk about these things, we bury them.

"Michelle was to be leaving the campus on a Saturday around noon, as soon as Ralph and Katie could get there. On Friday, another student said she saw Michelle going into the local post office with a letter and a small box. The letter, Dan, must have been the note she wrote to you."

Dan nodded.

"In the box was her diary, addressed to me. After that, none of the other students reported seeing her at all. They assumed she was alone in her room, packing her things. And from what I was told, none of them came to say good-bye. Or to wish her well. Or to say, here's my address, let's stay in touch. They were afraid her disgrace would rub off on them."

"Sounds to me like they were more afraid of this damn Barfy," Dan added. "Excuse me. Buffy."

"I can't help but wonder, if she heard one kind word, would she have changed her mind?" Claire asked. "Too late now. According to the medical examiner, she had been dead in that bath tub overnight before she was discovered. Meaning, she killed herself on Friday night."

"Oh, my Lord," George said. He had not known these details.

"Katie and Ralph arrived at about eleven AM the next day and were escorted to the headmistress's office. That's Miss Emch. Ralph was hiding how angry he was, but he could not do so for long. He didn't want to sit around and chat, he told the headmistress to have somebody go get Michelle and let's get her the Hell out of here.

"The headmistress called for a porter to go up to Michelle's room and get her things. But there was a problem locating him. It seems he was in the stable, waiting for the veterinarian. Something was wrong with one of the horses. It was very agitated and needed to be tranquillized."

"It was Whirlaway, wasn't it?" Dan asked.

"Yes. It was Whirlaway. He knew Michelle was dead, Dan. He *knew*, and his heart was breaking. But that created another delay which ticked off Ralph even more.

"Finally, the porter showed up. He found the room as neat as a pin, with Michelle's suitcases packed on her bed. But no Michelle. Miss Emch called the housemother and asked her to check the student lounges, the study hall, any other place Michelle might be. Still, no sign of her. Ralph was getting madder by the minute.

"Before she could call for another student to check the cafeteria and library, Ralph blew up. Cursing, swearing, shaking his fist at her, and announcing he would look for Michelle himself. Imagine this raging bull, trying to inspect these rich girls' sleeping rooms and closets and bathrooms. 'Mr. Casey, I'm afraid that will not be possible,' Miss Emch said. By that time, the porter had loaded their car with Michelle's belongings, and heard Ralph shouting. You know what rich people say? *Oh, Deah!* Such words are not allowed in the hallowed halls of St. Ethel's Academy. So, he called the police."

"Good thing for Miss Emch, he did," George observed.

"Well, maybe. The cops got there in record time. Since this was a Saturday, no one was in class. The students see all these squad cars pulling up in the driveway and get curious. They knew Michelle was supposed to be going home with her parents. A few of them, including this Buffy, decided to look around the dorm for her themselves.

"Buffy went alone into the bathroom. It was one of these communal bathrooms at the end of the hall. At one end, four toilet stalls. Sinks in the middle. At the other, three shower stalls, and one stall with a bath tub. Although the bathroom was deserted, that stall was locked from the inside.

"Buffy forced that stall door open. That's when she started screaming. You could hear her all over the campus. The cops came running up with their guns drawn. Followed by Ralph, Katie, Miss Emch and the porter. They all saw the horror of what was in there: Michelle, dead, immersed in her own blood.

"Now, at this point, Ralph really ran amok. Became totally hysterical. Even tried to lift Michelle out of the tub, while Buffy's shrieking away, and the cops are trying to get the scene sealed off. They had to force him out of the bathroom. But things are about to get worse."

"Hardly seems possible!" George and Dan agreed.

"Ralph was putting on quite a show. Out of control. How he loved Michelle, she was his whole life, he could not go on living without her. But he had to undergo questioning. And you, Dan, you know how that's done. Your books have shown us, often enough."

"Yes indeed," Dan said, "The Good Cop - Bad Cop scenario."

"You got it. Good Cop had no success. He was like, 'Mr. Casey, we know how hard this is, we want to help you but you must quiet down.'

"Bad Cop saw Ralph's hysteria as the load of BS it really was. He said something like this: 'The fact is, Mr. Casey, you were furious with your daughter because, in your eyes, she failed. When you got here, you had your wife engage Miss Emch in conversation, while you snuck up to your daughter's room. And you confronted her, Mr. Casey, you placed the blame on her. She denied that it was her fault. She was crying, Mr. Casey, and her tears were like a red cape to a bull. That's when you hit her, Mr. Casey. Pow! Right across her pretty face. She had it coming, didn't she? Didn't it feel good? So, you hit her again and again, harder and harder, until you knew she was almost dead. Then you dragged her down the hall, filled up the tub, cut her wrists with a razor blade, and left her to die if she weren't dead already.'"

"Sheeesh!" George said, "no wonder Ralph ran wild!"

"You know how it turned out," Dan added. "I had to go to the cops and the medical examiner with the letter Michelle sent me. Had Michelle been beaten before she died, there would have been other signs of external trauma. Bruising, broken bones. Her autopsy didn't show any. My letter, along with Michelle's diary, was proof that the cause of death was suicide. Not homicide, not an accident. And anything but natural."

"But Bad Cop did what he had to do, under the circumstances," Claire told them. "Ralph's out of control behavior created lots of suspicion. So, Bad Cop had to make sure that there was no foul play on Ralph's part. Or, if there was, to get him to confess. Ralph didn't see it that way, and never got over it."

"Incredible," was all George could say.

"Katie and Miss Emch and even the porter all had to be questioned," Claire told them. "Katie was useless. Again, her voice was gone. You know how she clams up. Refused to even speak one word."

"What became of Miss Emch?" George had to ask.

"Shortly thereafter, she resigned. There were a lot of hard feelings among the trustees about the publicity this generated. You should have seen those New York tabloids: *Bath Tub Horror at Posh Girls' School. Suicide Shatters St. Ethel's.* In her resignation letter, she said she could no longer pretend St. Ethel's was an academic sanctuary, when in fact it was a nest of snakes. She's teaching French somewhere in Florida, last I heard."

"And Buffy is shrieking on?" Dan asked.

"Yes, but not at St. Ethel's. Her grandfather put her in a private psychiatric facility. It's expensive, so it's called a sanitarium, as opposed to a nuthouse. She never got over what she saw. Frankly, I hope she never does."

"But there is still a St. Ethel's," Dan said, "and always will be."

"The rich you will always have with you," George added. "What was it, F. Scott Fitzgerald said to Ernest Hemingway?"

"'The rich are different from you and me,'" Dan told him. "To which Papa replied, 'yes, and they have more money.'"

"St. Ethel's no longer offers that scholarship program," Claire said. "If you're not rich beyond belief, you can't get in at all. Which is fine with me. But now you know how irrational Ralph can be. And why he will not allow any outside help to find Katie."

"That's what we're up against," Dan told George.

"And that's why…oh, I know Katie hates me," Claire said. "She can hate with a passion. She does not forgive the slightest offense. Mine was not slight. But I've been thinking: should I, as her sister, report her as missing? Take that responsibility myself?"

"No," said Dan. "Ralph's her next of kin. If he's not the one to do it, there will be even more Hell to pay. And he could call your search off."

"Thank you, Dan. And besides, if she were, well, dead, I think I would feel it. Somehow, I'd know."

"Do you?'

"She's alive. Out there somewhere. As of now I am certain. Jack Kennedy is dead, but Katie Casey is very much alive."

CHAPTER 18

Katie veered South into Tennessee. Hate guided her, stronger than ever. Hate was like a column of light, going before, showing her the way.

A column of light. The dragon led the ghosts in a circular dance around it, worshipping it. 'Twas the dragon, slayed John F. Kennedy, the way he...."

The way he slew someone else, whose name was locked in Katie's memory. This time, Katie put on the suit of armor and jumped on the steed. She would kill the dragon. And scatter the ghosts.

Soon she would cross Arkansas. Then, on into Texas. Then to Dallas and her destiny.

Her destiny: the total and utter destruction of Lee Harvey Oswald. Oh, how much he would suffer, for all the wrongs ever done to Katie Casey.

However, it seemed that perhaps her changing cars was not the wisest decision she had ever made. Thus far, there was no sign that anyone had followed her.

This heap was much more difficult to handle than her old car. The interior was dirty and reeked of tobacco. The upholstery was so worn it showed springs. The Engine Temp indicator kept creeping up. Above all, the mileage it was getting, even on the open highway, was terrible. There was no way Katie could get as far as Nashville without filling the tank. Again.

At least the radio somewhat worked. Katie could find NBC news as opposed to the preachers. And, Lord have mercy, the country western music. Her prey, Oswald, was in custody. He had killed a policeman as well as Kennedy, but would own up to nothing. He whined about his lack of legal representation. How unfairly he was being treated!

"I'll give ye something to whine about, ye little shite," she promised him in the words of her Irish ancestors.

Up ahead was a gas station. The attendant came out to wipe her windshield. He was a towhead mountain boy with a kind face.

"Fill it up. Regular," she told him.

"Check your oil, Ma'am?"

Katie had refused all previous offers to do this. Now it occurred to her, she had no idea when this heap last had an oil change.

"Well, actually, it's not my car," she explained. "It belongs to Dickie. My son, Dickie. Dickie always takes care of that. But, yes, and might I use your rest room?"

"Thataway. Don't need no key."

Katie would never have used this rest room, were she not on such an urgent mission. But she did, and went back out to her car.

"Ma'am?" the attendant asked.

"Yes?"

"Did Dickie tell you when he last had the oil changed?"

"Why, no. Is there a problem?"

"Well, now, I'd say yes. "This oil is in kind of bad shape. Been in there a good long while. And if you don't mind my sayin' so, there's other problems under the hood, could cause you some troubles down the line."

"I see," Katie replied.

Her mission was urgent. Her life would soon be over. "How much for the gas?" she asked.

"Two dollars and thirty-six cents."

Katie paid the exact change. "Ma'am, do you want me to…"

"Never mind," she replied. "I'll have Dickie look it over when I get home. Thank you for your help."

And she drove off, remembering his kind but puzzled face. At least the gas was cheap.

Katie did make it as far as Nashville. Of that she was certain, since a building she passed was marked GRAND OLE OPRY HOUSE.

She then had to turn into an area she considered bad. There was a Greyhound bus station, surrounded by lost-looking souls, of whom she disapproved.

She was eager to see the back of this place, when her whole mission nearly failed.

A scene came back to her, from *Gone with the Wind.*

Fleeing a burning Atlanta, Scarlett O'Hara had almost gotten herself, Melanie and Melanie's baby back to Tara. At which point, the nag Rhett Butler stole for them could do no more, and dropped dead.

If that car could speak, it would say in a soft Southern drawl, "Lawdy, Miz Scarlett, I cain't go on." The Engine Temp indicator was all the way up. White smoke billowed out from under the hood. The hood popped open and the radiator erupted like a volcano.

And it died, right in the street.

"What do I do now? Somebody tell me!"

Katie got her suitcases out of the trunk and wandered into the bus station. There was a bank of pay phones.

She was feeling dizzy, overheated and faint. Somehow, her sense of her divinely ordained mission grew dim. Who could help her?

Ralph. It had to be Ralph. He knew all about cars. Ralph would know what to do. What he did not know, his brother Jimmy did. Katie sat till she could catch her breath and entered a phone booth. The long-distance operator connected her to her home phone.

And it rang. Like it had yesterday. Rang and rang. By her bed. On the kitchen wall. No one picked it up. Who had been calling then, anyway?

'Ma'am, your party is not answering," said Long Distance Operator.

Katie hung up. A tear slipped from her eye. Was there no one who could help her?

She thought again of Scarlett O'Hara, who only wanted to return to Tara, wanted her mother. But wasn't her mission a lot more important? The future of the whole world was in her hands, as well as in the gun in her purse. All six slugs had to be delivered to Oswald's gut.

Was it really going to end like this? In a depressing bus station in Nashville, of all places? Then nothing made any sense!

Wait! No! Wasn't there someone else? Someone who had once shown her kindness, and would do so again if she would only ask him?

Again, Katie called Long Distance and asked for the city she never expected to see again.

"Name and address, please?"

"Daniel Doyle, 1410 Grimalkyn Lane."

"One moment, please."

Katie waited, feeling her mouth grow dry.

"Ma'am?" Long Distance said. "I'm sorry but the party's number is unlisted."

"Unlisted? What do you mean?"

"I'm sorry, Ma'am, I'm not allowed to give it out."

Katie banged the phone down. "You mean you're too damn lazy to do it," she muttered, and returned to her seat.

One of the ragged people was asking her if she was all right. "Yes, I am!" she snapped. "A good deal more than anyone!"

"I should have realized," she told herself, "Dan's rich and famous, and that's what rich famous people do. He can't be interrupted by some crazy fan in a bus station in Nashville."

Was there no other way to contact him? What about his New York publisher? But, no, that would take time she did not have. Besides, it was most likely that no one was there to take a call right now.

Where did that leave her? Another dizzy spell passed over her. An announcement came over the PA that boarding had begun for the next bus to Chicago.

Her vision grew dim and she nearly passed out. Then her eyes refocused.

She felt again like Scarlett O'Hara, realizing she had made it back to Tara, which was not burned like the other plantations. It still stood proud and tall, like her mission.

She saw a screen on the wall of pending departures. There was a bus leaving in a few hours for Dallas/Fort Worth. It would arrive early Sunday morning.

And she had enough for a ticket, too!

A sense of peace settled over her. This was meant to be. The world must be saved and she still had the means to save it. Katie Casey would not fail.

"Ha! Wouldn't Claire be sick with envy if she could only see me now?"

CHAPTER 19

On this gloomy Saturday, Dan's house seemed to be the place to go. Which was fine with him. Who would want to be by himself, on such a day as this? There were chips and dip, pretzels, beer, wine, soft drinks, really anything you could want. Several of the neighbors were there, including Frieda and Brunhilde. Even Father Gray, Claire's radical priest friend, stopped by with more good things to eat.

But it was not a happy occasion. In Washington, it was even darker and raining. Several of Dan's visitors wept when they saw Kennedy's rocker being carried out of the White House. Suddenly Frieda called out, Nein!

Brunhilde had been stealing pretzels. She gave Frieda her "who, me?" expression. It was agreed, let her have a few. Not the entire bowl, but a few!

Claire was in the back of the family room with Dan. On the schedule for today was a wake for dignitaries only, at the White House. Tomorrow there would be a public wake in the Capitol Rotunda. If Katie really was there, that would be the most likely time she would be seen on camera.

If, if, if.

"I just don't think she's there," Claire kept insisting. "And other things, too."

"What other things?" Dan asked her.

"The whole issue with Ralph's gun being missing. Where did it go? Who took it? For what?"

"Frieda's sure she heard Dickie tell Ralph he didn't know where it went."

"Yeah, right. Frieda's a reliable witness. But do you believe Dickie?"

"Now that you mention it, no."

"So, you think Dickie's carrying it?"

"What's the alternative?"

"Katie took it. Between the time you left her on that sofa, and the time Ralph and Dickie got home, there's a big window of opportunity."

"But you said she does not know how to use it."

"To the best of my knowledge, she doesn't. Recall, *I'm persona non grata.* And since Michelle died, she refuses to have anything to do with me. So, she may have learned how. I understand there are gun stores that offer classes for women only. I mean, I can't imagine Katie's taking one, but with her, there's no way to know. She's so secretive."

Claire lit a cigarette and took a deep drag.

"You think, then, Katie took the gun to Washington?"

"No, I'm thinking something a lot worse."

"What?"

"That she took it to Dallas."

There was a long pause, filled only with the commentary from NBC news. Then Dan said, "Oh, my dear Lord. Not there. It's like the OK Corral."

"I grew up with her, Dan. I know how her mind works. The slightest snub, and she will hate you for all eternity. She'll mull over it the way Brunhilde gnaws a bone. If she ever says, forgive us our trespasses as we forgive those who trespass against us, she means, don't bother to forgive me at all! Nobody can nurse a grudge like Katie. And the way she treats me? Like dirt, because I loved Michelle? Just the tip of the iceberg, Dan. So, watch out."

"She loves Jack Kennedy to the point of obsession."

"Oh, yeah," Claire nodded.

"And if anyone did him any harm…"

"She'd kill him."

"Oswald?"

"She intends to shoot him."

"You think she's capable of murder?"

"In this case? Yes, I do."

"How can she get him, Claire? Oswald's in police custody. Hell, he's probably the safest person in this country!" Then Dan added, to Father Gray, "Excuse me, I said Hell!"

"You're excused!"

"It's so far away. How would she get there?"

"Several ways. First: she could fly, but I'd question that because Katie's afraid of flying."

"Is that so?"

Claire nodded. "It's funny, but she's afraid of a lot of things. Being in an airplane is one of them. But don't scratch that. Yet. Second, she could take a train. If she picked either way, then her missing car is at the airport or the depot."

"Unless she decided to drive all way?"

"That's possible. But kind of improbable. Such a long way, through areas she has never been before. And she's not that good of a driver. Food Fair is about the only place she drives to, and she's never done a long-distance trip."

"What we could do is, check the parking lots at the airport and the depot for her car."

"It would be a start."

Dan agreed to go to the airport. George would check out the train station.

"Might I help out?" Father Gray asked.

"No, I think we have it under control."

"Remember," said Dan. "We're looking for a 1960 Chevy Bel Air four door sedan, white, plate number KT 1045. Oh, and there's a plaque on the back showing a pot of gold at the end of a rainbow, and Casey Chevrolet. Got it?"

George nodded.

"One more thing I just thought of," Claire added. She took a drag on her cigarette and had to laugh. "But it can't be! Can you even imagine Katie's royal Irish arse on a Greyhound bus?"

"I'll go to the Greyhound terminal!" Father Gray offered.

"Oh, thank you so much!"

The whole idea! It was crazy! But if it worked, it would at least be a start.

Claire settled on the couch beside Brunhilde, who wagged her tail. What a kind-hearted little dog she was.

If only the world had more Brunhildes, and less of this eternal hate. She recalled her former husband and his John Birch obsessions. And look what all this hate has given us. Just look at all the pain and sorrow.

There was something else on her mind. It came from seeing Dan and George cleaning up the kitchen together. For less than an instant, they exchanged a look between themselves.

Hate had nothing to do with it.

She and Dan had been friends since Michelle died, over a year ago. Unlike all the other men she had dated, he had never made a pass at her. (As had Ralph. Even after he married her sister. On more than one occasion.) Or demanded that she drop what she was doing and fix him a sandwich. Or asked to borrow a thousand dollars, which she would never see again. There was a pattern forming here.

Claire would say nothing of it. But at least these two souls loved each other. Hate had not won.

CHAPTER 20

Ralph had gotten lost several times. When Dickie took a turn driving, they got lost more often. By the time they reached Chevy Chase, Maryland, it was nearly dark and still raining. Ralph observed that the houses on both sides of the street looked expensive. There was even an elegant country club.

"Bet they won't let us in," Ralph speculated.

"Yeah," Dickie agreed.

Up ahead was a traffic circle with a fountain in the middle. Beyond that was the Welcome to Washington sign.

"We made it," Dickie said.

"Told you we would. Keep an eye out for your mother."

The more they progressed South on Connecticut Avenue, the denser traffic became. At one red light, they spotted a fat lady in a sidewalk crowd. Ralph rolled down his window and shouted, "Katie!"

She made no response. Ralph honked the horn and went on bellowing, "Katie! Katie!"

"Dad?"

"What?"

"That's not her."

A policeman came up to Ralph.

"Oh-oh," said Dickie.

"Sir, the president's dead. Could you please refrain from making that racket?" was all he asked.

"Sorry, um, I thought the fat lady was somebody else."

The light turned green. They passed the National Zoo, crossed a bridge, then went through an underpass.

"We must be near the White House," Ralph guessed. "If your mother's any place, that's where we'll find her."

"Yeah," was all Dickie said.

But they could not get near their destination. Ralph managed to park the car in an alley.

"You think it's all right to park here?" Dickie asked.

"Sure it is! Nobody will bother it," Ralph replied.

He and Dickie went on foot through a crowd in Lafayette Park. No one even resembled Katie. Cold rain kept falling.

"Gee, what do we do now?" Dickie asked.

Ralph sat on a bench, somewhat out of the rain, and gestured for Dickie to do the same.

"Here is where she's sure to be," Ralph said. "We wait."

Dickie sat beside his father in the chill rain, hoping they did not look too ridiculous. Like Abbott and Costello, or something. Besides, there were far too many crying girls in Lafayette Park for his comfort. He wished he were back on Grimalkyn Lane, in his warm bed, with his *Playboy* stashed between the mattress and springs.

Still, it did not pay to disagree with Ralph. Not here, not now.

On Grimalkyn Lane, George was the first to return. He had found nothing like Katie's car around the train depot.

Father Gray then returned and reported the same about the Greyhound station,

Last was Dan. He had checked out both short and long-term parking at the airport. Again, nothing.

"Oh, well," Dan said.

Claire looked up a map. The distance between Dallas and here was immense. "And Katie could be any place."

"It's getting dark," Dan added.

"OK," Claire decided, "No more wild goose chases. What happens, happens. As the song says, *que sera, sera.*"

"Whatever will be, will be," George added.

"Though when Katie's involved, rarely is it good."

Frieda and Brunhilde had gone home along with the other guests. Claire was going to go to Mass at Father Gray's place at eleven the following morning. Dan and Claire watched the endless news coverage as George put the food away.

The camera scanned the crowd in Lafayette Park.

"Hey, Claire!" Dan said. "Did you see that?"

"See what?"

"These two bums on the park bench. They looked like Ralph and Dickie."

"Where?"

"They're not on camera any more. I could have sworn. But, no, it can't be!"

Many hours later, and way behind schedule, the bus for Dallas/Fort Worth finally left the Nashville terminal. Katie was seething. This meant they'd be in Dallas late on Sunday morning. Didn't they understand the importance of what she had to do?

Apparently, not. At least she'd never have to take this bus again. Before leaving, she gave the station manager a piece of her mind. While boarding, she snarled at the driver.

Despite it all, it was good to be in her seat, better to be on the road. There was one major drawback. That car had a radio. She had been able to track Oswald's whereabouts. As for this bus, she would not want to borrow anyone else's transistor radio. Besides, it was so late, no one else would have wanted the darn thing on.

She knew that Oswald was due to be transferred from police headquarters to jail some time tomorrow. Best to strike while he was still between Point A and Point B.

Even if she missed that window of opportunity, there would be others. And she was not leaving Dallas until both she and Oswald were both in their caskets. That was a matter of fate.

CHAPTER 21

Ralph may have slept for a while on the bench in Lafayette Park. He dreamed of something that happened to him when he was thirteen.

This was in the big old house on Muratori Boulevard. Dad and his older brothers had taken everything out of the basement, to the back yard.

"We're going to get that ratty looking floor painted," Dad told Ma.

"That's nice. Who'd you hire?" Ma asked.

"I have eight sons, so I don't need to spend money on a painter."

"I want to do it, Dad!" Ralph insisted.

"No. You are too little. You are not mature enough. And you have not had enough experience."

"But I want to, Dad!" Ralph insisted. "I really want to! I watched you and Ben do the living room and I think I can do it. I really think so!"

The seven older brothers drew straws. Pete won the honor. "But, Dad!" Ralph whined. "I really, really want to! I'll show you I can do it! I'm not too little. And I am too mature enough."

"If that's what Ralph wants, it's OK by me," Pete said.

"Are you sure you know what you are doing?" Dad asked. "This is a big responsibility!"

"I can do it, Dad! I'll show you. You will be so proud of me."

"All right!" Dad sighed. "Give it a go!"

Ralph painted. Oh, how he painted! Around the basement steps, to the walls, and….

He had painted himself into a corner. There he stood, weeping.

Ralph remembered his father, standing on the basement steps, incredulous. "How could anyone with a dime's worth of sense do a thing like this?" Dad asked.

His brothers laughed at him. All of them, including Holy Joe.

Ralph did not remember how he escaped. His mother's pleas must have had a lot to do with it. Dad wanted him to stay in that corner till Hell froze over.

Then Ralph woke abruptly on the park bench. The sky was getting light. It was no longer raining but much colder. Dickie was still there.

"Did you find your mother?"

"No."

"She has to be here someplace!"

"She's not."

"Oh, for God's sake!" Ralph swore. "Let's go back to the car and get our stuff."

Dickie followed Ralph back to the alley. Their car was gone.

"Shit!" Ralph cried out. "It's been stolen!"

"Geez, and all our stuff's in it," Dickie added. "Even Mom's pills. Should we find a cop? There sure are plenty around."

"No, you fool!" Ralph began, then saw an official looking person who may well have been Secret Service.

"Excuse me, Sir," he said, suddenly as submissive as a stray dog to the alpha male of his pack. "A friend of ours parked his car in this alley last night and it seems to be missing. Could it have been stolen?"

"I can tell you one thing right off," the man said. "It wasn't stolen."

"It wasn't?"

"No, indeed! He left it there? He left it illegally. Parking there is illegal on an ordinary day. This is no ordinary day. It's been impounded. Here."

The man wrote down phone number. "Give him this. He can call and find out where it is. But he's going to have to pay a big fat fine to get it back. Plus, he most likely can't get it back till after the funeral. Look, we've got heads of state from all over the world. Security's a nightmare. We can't have strange cars all over the place. Have your pal call the number, that's all I can tell you." Then he made his way back to the White House.

Ralph stood on the sidewalk, holding the piece of paper, stunned.

"Dad?" Dickie asked.

Ralph turned on him, red-faced, and shouted, "You idiot! This is all your fault!"

CHAPTER 22

Dan and George both went with Claire to Sunday Mass at St. Mary Magdalen. They went early, since they expected the gang that never shows up except for Christmas and Easter to be there. They were right. As they walked in, they heard an old woman's voice call out:

"Claire? Claire Quinn?"

"Ma Casey!"

Dan and George watched as the two fell into each other's arms, weeping. Dan had to offer George a tissue.

"Aw, Ma, it's so good to see you! Even on such an occasion as this."

"And it's always such an occasion as this, isn't it?"

"Oh, here are my friends. You remember Dan?"

"Ah, yes. Something about the Battle of Gettysburg? Let me tell you, that book of yours sure was better than the movie."

"I'm glad you liked it."

"That I did. And this would be your half-brother George? From Peoria, is it? Yes, I do remember you!"

"Please to see you, Mrs. Casey."

"How are you holding up?" Claire asked.

"Ah! If it's not one tomfool thing, it's another. I presume you know, Katie's gone and flown the coop?"

"Oh, yeah, we know."

The old woman shook her head. "And so has Ralph."

"Here is what we heard," Claire offered. "That Ralph and Dickie think she went to Washington for the funeral, so they went after her."

"That, they did. Without a scrap of evidence, that they did. First funeral she's been to in how many years? And now they've gone and gotten into a peck of trouble."

"What did they do now?"

"Ralph parked their car in an alley near the White House. Then he and Dickie walked off to search for Katie on foot. Now, think about this. The place is crawling with the crowned heads of the whole world. Ralph dumps his car in an alley. What's the Secret Service going to think when they see that?"

Dan made a facepalm gesture. "Ka-boom, that's what they're going to think."

"So, Ralph goes back at dawn, looking for his car. Long gone, of course. Turns out it's been impounded. He can get it back, but sure and it will cost him an arm and a leg to do so."

"Has he got enough on him?" George asked.

"Absolutely not! And I certainly don't. He's been trying to call his brothers all morning, trying to get them to wire the money to the Western Union office."

"What did they say?"

"So far, the only one he's gotten hold of is Jimmy. Who told him to go to Hell."

Dan and George snickered.

"They had quite a conversation. Jimmy demanded to know, first off, if Katie's gone, why in God's name didn't you report her as missing? Especially if she's sick. Ralph made excuses. He can't get along with cops. Cops don't understand him. Jimmy said he's sick of hearing this. Said you've lost two whole days, you must start handling this like a mature adult and quit trying to play like you're The Goddam Lone Ranger. I am not paying for your stupidity. Go to Hell. End of conversation."

"Hi-yo Silver," George said to Dan.

"Silver's in the impound corral."

"Yeah, and I don't think Tonto's being too useful, Kemo Sabe."

"Woo!" said Claire. "What about the other brothers?"

"I haven't heard that he's succeeded in reaching any of them yet. Bishop Joe will be tied up most of the day. But of the lot of them, he'd be most likely to give in and wire the money."

"Let's hope he has sense enough not to give Ralph another free ride," Claire said, helping Ma Casey up the stairs and into a pew. Dan and George slid in beside them.

The mood was somber. Though the church was a good deal more crowded than it had been for Michelle, the service was the exact same. The memories were still present, still painful.

Eternal rest grant unto him, O Lord, and let perpetual light shine upon him. May John Fitzgerald Kennedy and the souls of all the faithful departed rest in peace. Amen.

One was a depressed teen. The other, the most powerful man on Earth. Both equal in God's sight, both unique and loved. Claire dabbed her eyes and wondered, why couldn't Katie have seen that? Why did she reject her own daughter, and dive head first into this inane fantasy romance? Just what was she running from?

They emerged into a bright and cold day. Claire assisted Ma Casey back into her car and promised to call her later. Then she joined Dan and George in a slow walk across the parking lot. At which point, the whole thing fell into another level of unreality.

There was Father Gray, still in his black vestments. "Claire. Dan. George. You can't leave yet. There's something you need to see. Come with me."

"What on Earth?" Claire asked.

"It's…it's about your sister," Father Gray was trying to explain.

"Katie's been found? Where?"

"No, not yet. Actually, it's not about her. You had expressed some apprehension that your sister had gone to Dallas. With the intention of shooting Oswald." He took them into a lower level room where there was a TV.

"Someone else just did."

"But that's impossible!"

"This was filmed not an hour ago," Father Gray explained.

The scene was of chaos in the Dallas police station. Someone was holding up a rifle.

"I can't look at that horrible thing," Claire said.

"You have to see what happens next," Father Gray told her.

Oswald. There he was, being transferred from the police station to jail. Her skin crawled. He could do no more harm. But he was surrounded by so many officials. He was, indeed, totally safe himself.

Until he wasn't.

Oswald shrieked in agony as the hot slug ripped up his gut.

Father Gray tried to explain, "You see? It was a man who did it. Not Katie Casey."

"Not my sister!" Claire wept. "Thank you, God, not my sister!"

CHAPTER 23

Katie was remembering, as the Dallas-bound bus rolled through the night.

She had been about twelve, eating her lunch in the school cafeteria, when she saw Loretta Keene approaching. *Oh-oh,* she thought. Katie loathed Loretta intensely.

Loretta was the glamor girl in her class, always reading *Photoplay* and copying the styles of real movie stars. Her life plan was to become an actress. She really did move to Hollywood after high school. No one ever heard from her again. Katie was pleased to think that Hollywood chewed her up and spat her out.

"I just wanted to tell you, I saw your father in the park on Sunday. He was with a pretty lady."

"So what?" Katie asked.

"So, I don't think she was your mother. Does your mother know about her?"

"Like, that's any of your business?" Katie snapped. "She must be one of his clients, that's all."

"Does he always hold hands with his clients?"

"Get lost," Katie advised her. "Go play in traffic."

"I'm only trying to be helpful," Loretta whined, but at least she left.

The following Sunday after Mass, Katie snuck upstairs and changed from her best dress to a scruffy shirt and pants. She pinned up her hair, put on a cap, and admired herself in the mirror. Any casual observer would mistake her for a boy. Then she set off for the park.

Sure enough, there was her father with Mrs. Keller, together on a bench. There was an ice cream stand close by. He got up to purchase two cones.

While his back was turned, Katie ran behind the bench, tipped it over backwards, and dashed into the woods. Her victim never had time to scream. There was a loud *crack* as Mrs. Keller's head hit the concrete curb.

Once Katie reached the top of a hill, she hid behind a tree to look back. There was a puddle of blood underneath Mrs. Keller's head. Her father had dropped both ice cream cones and was shouting, "Rose! Darling! Speak to me!" A crowd was gathering.

"I saw it!" someone said. "It was one of those nasty boys from the orphanage!"

"Tee hee!" Katie laughed as she ran all the way home.

She never did tell anyone, not Mother, not Claire, not even Ralph. Neither did she ever speak of this in Confession. Katie lurched in her seat.

Even on this lowly bus, it was good to have a window seat. Now that the sun was up, Katie studied the terrain she was passing through.

Flat. So terribly flat. This must be Texas.

Katie felt inside her purse for the gun. It was still there. She smiled. It would not be long now.

Some of the other passengers were awake, moving around. Katie glared out the window. She wasn't about to speak to any of the others on this bus.

Though you might not know it to look at her, she was the most important person in this world. Someday she'd be in all the history books as the one who avenged John F. Kennedy. Why, she would even be held up as a role model for twelve-year-old girls. What would her family think then?

She saw herself reflected in the window. Oh, dear. She must look as bad as anyone else on this miserable bus. That was not the sort of image she'd want in a history text. It would be better to use a picture from the time before she married Ralph, had children, gained so much weight. Her engagement portrait might be better. *Katherine Marie Quinn Casey, 1921 – 1963.* If only there were a way to make her wish known.

Still, Katie would be remembered as the one who saw the problem, then had the gumption to solve it. The rest chose to live with it. Like a flock of bleating sheep.

She thought of Ralph, wondering where he was now. It still troubled her that when she got off this bus, he'd be waiting there. He'd say, "Honey, don't do this, it's not worth it."

But it was! If he were there, she'd get away from him. If he ran after her, she'd tell the Dallas Police he was a strange man, bothering her. No, she was not his wife, he's crazy!

Ralph might try to say, "Give me the gun and let's go home. We'll never talk about this again."

Then the whole thing would be banished, forgotten, buried.

Like Michelle.

There was no way that was going to happen. *Ralph, don't follow me, I'm going to be dead soon. But suppose he had already reported her as a missing person? Or suppose he had hired a private detective?*

Unlikely. They were said to charge a lot and she knew how Ralph felt about that. Still, it paid to be vigilant.

She would leave the bus terminal as quickly as she could and proceed at once to Oswald's last known location. Then she would act. Quite possibly, it would all go down today. Then she would be dead. *What was it like, to be dead?* Up till now, the thought had repelled her.

And was there anything else she wanted to say, while she was still alive?

To Ralph? No.

To Dickie? "Your mommy loves you very much; be a good boy for me."

To Claire? "I hate you! Michelle was my daughter, not yours, you had no right to do anything for her. Not after she threw away the life I gave her. That made her nothing and nobody."

Somehow, the thought of being dead did not disturb her at all. She continued to gaze out of the window at the endless flatness of Texas. There was nothing left but the low growl of the engine and the endless turning of wheels.

***

Ralph and Dickie had made their headquarters a pay phone outside the Western Union office. They were running low on change. Thus far, the only one of his brothers he'd spoken with was Jimmy.

And Jimmy told him where to get off at. Hah! Just for that, he'd buy his next car at McCormick Ford, and see how Jimmy liked that. Two can play at this game.

Mostly, no one answered when he called. Paul's youngest son had picked up the phone, but he was three years old and did not know what he was doing. "Go get your mommy!" Ralph ordered him. "Now!"

"Is dis Bozo de Clown?" the kid asked.

"No!" Ralph snarled, and scared the boy so much he hung up wailing.

Ralph and Dickie sat on the curb. Ralph could not hit up Ma again, she didn't have that kind of money. Thus far, the only hopeful call they had made was to Bishop Joe's office. It was answered by a secretary, but at least, it was answered.

No, His Excellency was not in, and would most likely be unavailable for the rest of the day. Ralph left the number of the pay phone. "And tell him it's a goddam emergency!"

Only now did he regret his choice of words. He remembered when he was a small boy. Holy Joe used to pretend to say Mass, to consecrate Uneeda biscuits and Coca-Cola in sing-song Latin. Ma forced his brothers to be his congregation. However, since Joe's back was turned to his flock, he never knew half of what went on in the pews.

"What do we do?" Dickie asked.

"We wait," said Ralph. "Then we call 'em all again and reverse the charges."

"Suppose they don't accept?"

"They damn well better."

They waited. The wind became colder.

"Dad," said Dickie, "Listen!"

"For what?"

Ralph heard the clip-clop of horses' hooves on pavement. Then the loud *Boom! Boom! Boom!* of drums, echoing down the urban canyon.

"It's starting," Ralph whispered. "They're taking him to the Capitol."

Dickie just sat. He would remember that sound. It would haunt him for the rest of his life, even in Viet Nam. They almost did not hear the pay phone ringing.

Ralph picked it up and said, "Yeah?"

"Ralph, Ralph, Ralph," said Holy Joe. "What am I going to do with you?"

"Joe! I'm in a real mess now. And Jimmy told me to go to Hell! Can't you excommunicate him or something?"

"The fact that Jimmy told you to go to Hell, did not obligate you to take his words literally. What's that thundering in the background?"

"They're taking Kennedy's body to the Capitol."

"Jesus, Mary and Joseph. Have mercy on his soul."

There was a pause.

"Joe?" Ralph asked.

"Ma called me earlier. Ma told me what you and Dickie went and did."

Another pause.

"And I remembered. When you were thirteen. And Dad let you paint the basement floor."

Ralph groaned.

"Now, any normal person would have started with the corners, and worked his way toward the stairs. But not you. You painted over your escape route first. Then into the corner. Didn't you stop and think?"

"Joe, please!"

"And now you've done the exact same thing again."

Another pause.

"All right," said Joe. "I recall that the whole thing struck me as funny. At the time. It wasn't. You really were too little to take on such a big job all by yourself. Maybe Pete should have been your assistant, I don't know. I regret having laughed at you. It was wrong. I know this comes late, but please forgive me."

"Um, yeah," said Ralph.

"Here is your present situation as I understand it. When you got home on Friday, Katie was gone."

"Yes."

"Did she leave a note? Or any word as to where she was going?"

"No."

"Did you look for her?"

"Yes, everyplace! She woke up that morning sick, she's supposed to be taking medication, only she left her pill bottle behind."

"Did you report her to the authorities as missing?"

"No."

"May I ask, why not?"

"Because…because…you know, they're not supposed to do anything for, what, three days, is it?"

"I don't think that's quite true. Especially in the case of a sick person, but go on."

"Look, Joe. I'm not going to go to the cops again. Not after the way I was treated when Michelle died. They acted like I was a crook! Like they thought I murdered her. You know, it was an accident. It was not my fault! She fell in the tub and drowned!"

The bishop sighed. "Ralph, pull yourself together. That was a terrible thing, yes, but you made it so much worse by losing control of yourself and going on a rampage. Please don't do it now."

Ralph sniffled.

"That's better. Now, you and Dickie acted on the assumption that Katie went to Washington alone, for the president's funeral?'

"It made sense."

"You parked your car illegally and found out the following morning that it had been impounded. Where did you spend last night?"

"On a bench in Lafayette Park."

"Lord, have mercy," said Bishop Casey.

Another pause.

"And I presume you have not found Katie."

"Not yet. It's kind of crowded here. But…"

"But nothing. Listen closely. There is something I can do for you. But it's not going to be for free. Here is what you must do. First, report Katie as a missing person."

"Um, here? Right now?"

"I can see that you have a problem. The Washington police have their hands full. Will you give me your consent to report Katie as missing to the authorities here?"

"Joe, I really don't want you doing that. I don't want them involved. I really think Dickie and I can find her ourselves."

"Thus far, your efforts have been less than a spectacular success."

Another pause.

"You and your son have lost your car and all your possessions in it, you are living on the street, and I gather you are almost out of funds, am I right?"

"We're a little short, yeah, but…"

"We're down to our list dime," Dickie muttered.

"Ralph, this can't go on. Not just for your sake, but Katie's. Recall, this is not about you. This is about Katie. You don't know where she went, you know she has health problems, and Ma did mention she loved President Kennedy? She may well be taking his death very hard?"

"Well, yeah."

"I can help you, Ralph. But only if you let me. First, you stop looking for Katie on your own and give me your consent as her next of kin, to report her as an endangered missing person. Promise me that once I do so, you will do nothing to call the search off."

"What's second?"

"We have to get you and Dickie into a safe place before you both get pneumonia. If you are sick yourself, you will be of no use to Katie. Now, I understand you have no chances of getting a hotel room right now. I am going to arrange to put you up in a monastery. Write down this address. It's in Northeast Washington, a section called Little Rome."

Ralph wrote it down. "Where's he putting us?" Dickie asked.

"In a suite at the Mayflower!" Ralph snapped. "With room service!"

"You can stay until you can get your car out of the impound lot, even if you do have to wait till the funeral is over. Then you and Dickie must come home with no further delay."

"Yeah, but how can I get the car without paying the fine?"

"How much is the fine?"

Ralph told him. Again, the bishop called upon Jesus, Mary and Joseph.

"Oh, Joe? One other thing."

"And what might that be?"

"Well, um, I kept a gun in the nightstand. Only it wasn't there when I looked for it. So, it's gone missing, too."

"It's missing, too," Joe repeated. "Ralph, to your knowledge, is it loaded?"

"Um, yeah. That's how I left it."

"And you think Katie took it?"

"I really don't know."

"Does she know how to handle it safely?"

"No. She does not."

"In which case, she may be armed. I am going to have to include that when I file the missing person report. Do you realize this makes the whole situation a lot more volatile?"

"Um, yeah, I guess so."

"You guess so?"

"Does this mean you can't help me?"

"Ralph, for pity's sake. If you agree to all I have asked you to do, I will wire those finds to the Western Union office, plus a bit more to get you home safely."

"You will?"

"Please understand, this is not a gift. This is a loan. It must be paid back in full as soon as you get back. I'm going to have to dip into some church funds, and you know how Cardinal Bean Counter feels about that. Do you agree to that, Ralph? Do we have an understanding here?"

"You really can do this for me?"

"Yes. With all the stipulations. Father Albert is the abbot there. He is going to call me when you and Dickie arrive. But, yes, if you hold up your end."

"You got a deal, Joe. I swear to God, you got a deal!"

"I'd thank you to go easy on the swearing."

Ralph and Dickie had to take a DC Transit bus to Little Rome. "We have been expecting you," Father Albert greeted them. They were given a monk's spare cell, clean clothes, and decent meals. Even though the real monks refrained from watching TV, Ralph and Dickie were permitted a small one with the volume low. They could catch up on the news they had missed all day.

"This sure ain't the Mayflower," Dickie observed.

"Stuff it," was Ralph's advice.

They watched the black and white image of Oswald being lead out of the Dallas police station. There was that rifle again in the background.

"Look at those eyes on him. One cunning mean bastard," said Ralph.

Then came the loud bang, the agonized scream. Dickie's "Oh, shit!" echoed down hallowed corridors.

CHAPTER 24

Back at Dan's house, Claire was in need of a cup of tea. "And a few dozen tranquillizers, if you guys have any."

"We seem to be out," said Dan. "Oh, never mind the tea. How about a good stiff drink? Old Grand Dad appeal to you?"

"I'd better stick to tea. I need my mind clear. Though getting drunk now does have a certain appeal. It will have to wait."

"You've had a big shock," Dan said. George turned on the news.

"What are they saying?" Dan asked him.

"It was a man. Acting alone. Jack Emerald, I think his name was, don't quote me on that."

"Don't worry, I won't."

"Oswald's in Parkland."

"How ironic," was all Dan could say.

Claire then called Ma Casey. Yes, she saw the same gruesome scene on live TV. "Oh, and I heard from Bishop Joe. Ralph managed to hit him up."

"What did Joe say?" Claire asked, "Please go to Hell, do not pass Go?"

"No, he wired the funds to Ralph. Provided Ralph pays back every thin dime, right away. And with a big stipulation."

"What's the stipulation?"

"Ralph has to stop this silly escapade immediately, stop looking for Katie on his own. Ralph agreed."

"What, did Joe threaten him with the tortures of the Inquisition?"

"He didn't have to. Ralph was cold, tired, hungry, in a city where he does not know anyone. He's not used to that. Having Dickie along is no help. Oh, and Joe wants them both in a safe place, so he put them in a monastery till they can get their car and come home."

"Wait. Are you telling me that Ralph and Dickie are in a *monastery?*"

"I know, I know, it's a bit beyond belief, isn't it?" Ma asked. "Above all, Ralph had to give Joe his consent as Katie's husband, to report her as an endangered missing person. Which is where I come in, I'm afraid."

"How so?"

"Joe says the police need more information on Katie. They have a pretty good description: white female, blue eyes, short light brown hair, 5'8" height. Weight, we are not too sure of. Two hundred pounds, a least, likely more."

"Quite possibly, closer to two-fifty."

"One other thing in the report. Subject may be armed; approach with caution. As for her car, we have 1960 Chevrolet Bel Air 4 door sedan, white, plate number KT 1045 and a Casey Chevrolet plaque in back."

"Sounds right."

"But they need more. They need some recent close-up pictures of Katie. And I'm afraid I don't have too many. I'm looking through what I do have. Mostly pictures of that ghastly wedding, and they are not too recent."

"I wish I could help, Ma, but most of the pictures I have are of the two of us together, and we're still little kids."

"Do you know of any markings she might have, like tattoos?"

"Katie, with a tattoo? None too likely."

"Any surgical scars?"

"None that I know of. You know, Ma, we need to get our heads together on this," Claire suggested.

"Have Ma Casey come on over," Dan said.

"Can you come over to Dan's house? It's right across the street from Ralph's."

"Expect me shortly!"

"Guys?" George asked,

"What fresh Hell is this?" Dan asked him.

"I don't think Oswald's going to make it. Not with a slug in his gut."

"What did I tell you?" Dan reminded them. "It's the fecking OK Corral, all over again. And it does not look make us look good."

CHAPTER 25

Many hours behind schedule, the Greyhound from Nashville pulled into the Dallas/Fort Worth terminal. Katie had a hard time, rising from her seat. The driver she had snapped at offered to help her down the stairs. She refused his help.

"I don't need you," she snarled.

The fact was, Katie Casey did not need anyone. She was just a bit unsteady on her feet, that was all, from having to sit for so long.

She saw her suitcases being unloaded. Unlike her fellow passengers, who were picking up their own bags, she decided to abandon hers here at the terminal.

"I'll not be needing it where I'm going." If these sad sacks wanted her things, they could pick through them. She had her purse and sure enough, Ralph's gun was still in it.

Katie took a quick look at a map. Oswald was last known to be in the police station. She'd go there first. But it was a bit of a distance, she did not know the Dallas bus system, and she was too low on cash for a taxi.

Well, she'd find it. Her whited-hot hate for the little bastard had guided her thus far. And three was no sign that Ralph or Dickie or anyone she knew was waiting for her.

Good!

Katie left the terminal. She still felt a little dizzy. Perhaps being out in the open air, and off that bus, would help clear her head.

The terminal was in a poor part of Dallas. Katie walked on. This seemed to be the correct direction to the police station. Yet, somehow, things did not look right. As if they were not real. Or drifting in and out of reality.

Keep going. You are almost there.

Her surroundings no longer appeared poor and shabby. In fact, this looked like a much better area. There were high-rise office buildings and luxury hotels. People passing her on the street were clean and well-dressed. They looked important. Unlike Katie, they knew where they were going.

Katie sat down on a bench outside a hotel. There was a large plaza with a splashing fountain.

"This is…this is…" Katie spoke to herself. "Lots of money. But not like St. Ethel's. There they, they, they, had old money. Here they have, have, have, what? What is the word I need? Old? No! Oil! That's it! Oil money! That's what I'm looking at! Oil! Money!"

"Are you all right? Do you need any help?

Katie looked up. There was a beautiful young woman, towering over her.

Danger! Danger!

Katie saw a red light flashing inside her head. The woman was wearing a full-length mink coat.

"You lying bitch!" Katie shouted. With her left hand, she grabbed onto this woman's mink.

"Oh, excuse me, I'm sorry. I didn't mean to upset you."

"You. In. That. Coat."

The words were so slow to come.

"Please!" the stranger begged. "I meant no harm, please let me go!"

"You. Lied! Your. Lies! You. Hurt. One. I love. This. Is. For. You, Buffy Van Hooper!"

Saying so, she spat into this stranger's face. The mink-clad woman screamed, "Harry! Somebody help me!" She tried to get out of Katie's grip. Her only chance of escape was to wiggle out of her coat and let Katie have it. She ran into the hotel lobby, screaming for Harry.

Katie dragged the mink over to the fountain and heaved it in. She laughed as it grew heavy and sank to the bottom.

"Too bad! Ask Grandpa to buy you another one."

"Harry!"

Katie staggered into the hotel. She could not find her victim but heard her still screaming for Harry, to rescue her. Everyone else was heading into the Longhorn Bar, which had a large screen TV.

"They're bringing him out!" someone said. "Oswald!"

"Any minute!"

"Here he comes!"

"Sarah!" a man called to his wife. "Over this way, you have to see this!"

Katie tried to find her victim in the crowd, but there were many women in mink coats. Many Buffies.

"You. Hurt. My. Michelle. So. Much. It. Was. You. Killed. My. Baby. Girl. My little Mimi."

Katie tried reaching into her purse with her right hand. It did not seem to be working but the left one grasped Ralph's gun.

The image on the TV changed. Everyone else in the bar looked up at it. "We now take you live to Dallas Police Headquarters, where Lee Harvey Oswald is about to be transferred to an armored car."

"Can you believe this?" someone asked.

Again, a crowd of men filled up the screen. Someone was holding up Oswald's rifle.

And there he was. Grinning at Katie, saying, *yes, I did it, what are you going to do about it?*

There was an explosion, and the entire television burst a shower of glass shrapnel. Screams and panic broke out at the bar. Blood gushed from open head wounds. Others, trying to escape, blocked all possible exits. Patrons seated at the bar sustained the worst injuries.

Katie did not stop shooting till all six chambers were empty, destroying the TV and many bottles of costly whiskey. Then she fell to the floor, trying to say something.

Perhaps it was *Sic Semper Tyrannis.* Or perhaps it wasn't. Katie Casey had said all she intended to say. Let the record show.

CHAPTER 26

"Where do we stand?" Claire asked Ma Casey.

"Here's what I've got. Their wedding album."

"Any other pictures of Katie?"

"Just these, and they're not very good."

Ma handed Claire a pile of pictures from last Christmas. "Katie never wanted her picture taken. Her weight embarrassed her."

In every picture where Katie appeared, she was turning away from the camera. "I don't think the cops can use these," Claire said. "Where do you think we can find better ones?"

"That's easy," said Ma, indicating the house across the street

"Won't we have to break in?"

Ma reached into her purse and pulled out a key. "Michelle's."

"But they're not home yet."

"Sure, but being Ralph's Old Ma, it might not be too terribly illegal for me to walk on in."

"I'd better come with you," Claire offered. "We might have to get up in the attic, and I don't want you on those pull-down stairs."

"You need us to come with you?" Dan asked

"I think you really don't want to be back in there," Claire told him. "Besides, it might be better if you and George stayed here. Keep an eye on the screen. If you see anyone who looks like Katie, write down the location, and at what time."

"Sounds like a good idea."

"Oh, one other thing," Claire said. "Dan, do you have a pair of dishwashing gloves?"

"Sure. You want to avoid dishpan hands?"

"Nope. I don't want to leave any of my prints over there."

"I don't have to worry about that," said Ma. "Let's hope Ralph didn't change the locks."

"I very much doubt he'd want to pay for that," Claire replied. "Here goes nothing."

Dan watched Claire and Ma cross Grimalkyn Lane. Ma put Michelle's key in the lock and the door popped open. Ma flashed him a V sign.

"They're in like Flynn," Dan said. "Any Katie sighting yet?"

"No," said George. "Jackie. Caroline. Sad beyond belief. But no one looks like Katie. You know what I think this is? On Katie's part?"

"What?"

"Attention-getting behavior."

"How so?"

"Well, think about it. Like you said. Katie rarely goes anywhere. Or associates with anyone."

"She isolates herself."

"And why do you suppose she does that? To call attention to herself, is why."

"Conspicuous by her absence."

"Right! People notice she's not there, and that way, she's the center of attention."

"Because she couldn't be, if she actually showed up?"

"That's it. And you know something? It works."

"Thus, the behavior is reinforced and she keeps doing it. I mean, look at the parties in the Wagners' back yard. Always fun. Especially with Brunhilde. But Katie either has an excuse for not going. Or, if she does go, she sits in a corner by herself, won't talk to anybody, leaves early. Like she's miserable."

"Of course, she's miserable! The party is not all about her."

"That's really pathetic."

"But maybe she's happy now. Because she sure has everyone's attention. At least, around here."

"Where do you think she is now, George? What do you think she's up to?"

"I wish I knew. But at least the missing person report has been filed. It's out of Ralph's hands. And that ought to account for something."

"Claire has a theory. That something really bad happened to Katie when she was a kid only no one will talk about it. This happened when Claire had polio. I think she was about four. Katie would have been about seven."

"Could well be, whatever it was, she's still having issues with it. Mommy sounds miserable. Daddy's busy cheating on her."

"Maybe it's some sort of abandonment issue."

"So, Katie will abandon you, rather than risk your abandoning her."

"Whatever," Dan admitted. "All we can do is speculate."

"Which we do so brilliantly."

Across the street, Claire and Ma decided to start at the top and work their way down. First, they lowered the attic stairs. "Wait here, Ma," Claire told her, and squirmed through the attic entrance, then reached down for the flashlight Ma passed up.

"Somebody's been up here recently," Claire called down.

"Why do you think so?"

"Everything's covered with dust, but there are fresh footprints on the floor."

"Katie's? You think she's been hiding there all this time?"

"Whoever did this was a man. Big fellow, big feet. Ralph or Dickie, most likely. But if Katie were up here, she would have strangled me by now."

"What else do you see?"

"A decapitated head."

"What on Earth?"

Claire tossed a doll's head down to Ma. "This used to be mine. It was a Baby Jane doll. Mom had Katie give it to me when I got home from the hospital."

"In 1928?"

"Yep. Katie resented it. One day I went looking for Baby Jane and she was gone. Katie swore up and down that she had no idea where the doll was. I should have known it would be up here. I wonder where the rest of Baby Jane went?"

Ma thought of Hamlet, holding Yorick's skull.

"Oh, no," Claire signed.

'What is it?"

"Michelle. All Michelle. Even her guitar. It's broken beyond repair. This is the place where she was exiled and forgotten."

Claire picked up a St. Ethel's uniform wool blazer, badly moth-eaten, with the crest hanging off it.

"That's all?"

"No. Wait. There are some photo albums here."

Claire passed them down, then managed to get back down and re-close the attic stairs. "These might yield something."

"Maybe. Now let's look in their bedroom."

"What a mess!" Ma exclaimed. Katie's underwear had been heaved all over the place. Ex-large panties hung from the ceiling light fixture.

"There is a reason for some of the mess. Long story. Dan knows it."

"Like one of his own stories?"

"Better. But as for the rest of the mess, I cannot figure out, for the life of me, why my sister would want to live like this. Did these sheets ever get changed? This ought to be reported to the Board of Health. I thought they had a maid."

"They did," said Ma. "Avocet. Ralph got rid of her."

"Too cheap, is that it?"

"Partly. Ralph was paying her practically nothing. She wanted a raise, and to clean a place like this, she deserved it. But Avocet wanted something else, too."

"What was that?"

"Time off to get to the big rally in Washington at the end of August. Martin Luther King was going to make a speech. Word on the street was, it was going to be the speech of his life. Her heart was set on being there for it."

"I'll bet that got on Ralph's last nerve."

"It did. He pulled a dirty trick on her. He gave her the raise she wanted. And the time off. But when she came back from the rally, guess what? No more job."

"What a rotten thing to do!"

"Avocet was a good cleaner. She never would have let this place get into this state, that's for sure."

"Let's see what we've got so far."

Most of the photo albums were years old, but the most recent one had a few pictures of Michelle and Katie on the campus of St. Ethel's.

"Ralph must have taken these," Ma observed. "This was just after Michelle won her scholarship and they were given a tour of the campus. Looks good, doesn't it?"

"A little too good," said Claire. "Even the shrubs don't look alive. They're too perfect. Like they must be fake, not real. But there are some good ones of Katie's face here. And I doubt we'll find anything more recent."

"We'll take them to Joe's office, then."

"One other thing," Claire said, and slowly opened the nightstand with her gloved hand. "Ralph was right," she told Ma. "There's no gun in here."

"Nor should there have been. He lied to me, Claire. He told me he got rid of it, years ago."

"But Dan was here Friday, trying to help Katie. He saw it. Right there. And now it's gone."

"Ralph knew how I felt about that gun, loaded and ready to go off, in an unlocked drawer, with two children in the house. Michelle was despondent sometimes, even before St. Ethel's, because of the way Ralph treated her. His favorite was Dickie. And Dickie never did have a dime's worth of sense. I told Ralph, that gun is a tragedy, waiting to happen. He agreed with me. He told me, he put an ad in the paper and sold it years ago. And now, this. What's in that box in the back of the drawer?"

Claire opened it up. "Extra ammo. We can be glad that Katie forgot it."

Ma sat on the bed.

"I tell you, I'm getting too old for this. Ralph is the only one of my boys who could not get his life on track. And, Katie? I never did like or trust her. It's true, I needled her about her weight. But beyond that, she was so selfish. Everything had to be about her, or she picked up her marbles and went home. There are times, well, times I wished he'd married you, Claire, even though you were the younger one, and such things were not done to single older sisters. Especially if they were not attractive. Maybe you could have changed him, I don't know."

"Ma," said Claire, "I could no more change Ralph, than I could sober up an alcoholic, by marrying him. It doesn't work. Too many have tried it. And it never works."

"I know, Dear. But I wish. I wish. Let's get these pictures to Joe. I just hope we don't see them on a wall at the Post Office, if you get my meaning."

"I do, Ma."

The left, carefully locking the door behind them. Dan took Ma in the Porsche to the bishop's office with the pictures. The Casey house was again dark and silent. Even the roaches under the kitchen sink did not stir.

Then the phones jumped to life. The one on the nightstand was crying out as if in distress to the one on the kitchen wall, which cried back to it.

Ring! Ring! Help me, help me!

No one was at home to answer.

CHAPTER 27

Katie opened her eyes. At least, the left eye. The right one seemed to be stuck open. She tried to speak.

"Where are you?" a nurse asked, "You're in Parkland Hospital, in Dallas. Mrs. Casey, isn't it?"

Someone else whom she could not see spoke and said: "We've got a Social Security card and an out-of-state driver's license, both for Katherine Casey."

No! No! Katie tried to say but the words did not come out. I'm not Katherine Casey. My name is Katherine Kennedy. You found my driver's license and Social Security card? They are easily explained. I just got married so I have not had time to get them changed yet. But I will, as soon as we're back from our honeymoon. We're at a secret location, where gentle waves break on a white sandy beach. There are palm trees swaying in the breeze. Birds of Paradise call to each other. Oh, to stay here forever! But Jack has to get back to running the country.

Others spoke: "There's an address here. 1409 Grimalkyn Lane."

"Call information, see what they have."

That's wrong! My new address is 1600 Pennsylvania Avenue, Washington DC. You won't find anyone at that old address. The house was sold and they all went away. Ralph, Dickie, all of them. Jackie went away too. She took her kids and ran off with her friend, that nice Mr. Onassis.

"Mrs. Casey, can you hear me? Do you understand me? Do you recall what happened before you came here?"

My name is Katie Kennedy.

"It appears that you have had a stroke. But this is very important: do you remember anything else you did today?"

Katie used her left arm to try to get up. "No, Ma'am, you can't leave. See, you are in a unit for persons who have been arrested."

I have never been arrested! My name is Katie Kennedy.

"Excuse me, Doctor," the nurse said. "He just died."

"Oswald?"

"Afraid so."

"Mrs. Casey, I'll be right back." Someone just inches from her was being wheeled away. Within reach! Katie again tried to rise and with her left hand, grasped the sheet that covered Oswald's body. She tore it off his face. Yes, it was the one that had been mocking her. Now it was frozen in agonizing pain.

Katie Casey spat in that face.

The sheet was pulled from her hand and placed back on Oswald. "Whoa! Mrs. Casey! Please don't do that!"

There was more shouting in the corridor. Two women were wailing and lamenting, one in English, the other in Russian. A baby cried.

Someone plunged a needle into Katie's arm. She was transported into a Dan Doyle sequel, helpless on a ship, trapped in a vortex spinning round, spinning down, *to the last I grapple with thee, from hell's heart I stab at thee; for hate's sake, I spit my last breath at thee.*

Then the ocean closed over her. There were only the cawing seabirds left.

One of them screeched that they had a perfectly good phone number, but no one answered at that location.

CHAPTER 28

Monday morning had arrived, and with it, the president's funeral. Ralph had already had one call from Bishop Joe.

"You and Dickie stayed all night at the monastery?"

"Yeah."

"Good. Now the important thing is that you stay put all day. You can watch the ceremonies on TV. But don't leave the monastery grounds, and above all, don't get into any more trouble. Is that clear, Ralph?"

"Um, yeah."

"And in the morning, go get your car and drive right back here. Call me the minute you get back."

"Yeah. Um, have you heard anything about Katie?"

"Your mother found some good pictures of her. We may have had a sighting of her. But it was nowhere in the Washington area."

"Where was it, can you tell me?"

The bishop sighed. "At a gas station near Nashville, Tennessee."

"Nashville! Why in the Hell, excuse me, why would Katie go to Nashville?"

"That, we don't know. And the witness was not too sure. His description sounded like Katie. And he remembered that she spoke of a son named Dickie. But she did not offer him her name, and she paid in cash for her gas. And his description of her car was totally different from Katie's. It had Kentucky plates."

"So, it's probably a bum lead. I thought so. Nashville, she wouldn't go there."

"Probably so. But be assured, we have professionals looking for her. And I will let you know right away, should we get a better lead today."

Dickie, in the humble cell, had been watching the funeral march, hearing the haunting drums. He had been thinking.

Indeed, this monastery was nothing like a ritzy hotel. But it wasn't bad. In fact, he had come like it a bit. He tried to figure out why.

He and Ralph had little contact with the monks. But what he saw of them, they seemed like cool guys. Awfully quiet, but nice.

Then it dawned on Dickie, why he liked it here. There were no women. Therefore, no weeping teenage girls to creep him out.

Ralph returned from his phone call. For a while, they watched the grim march: Bobby, Jackie, Teddy, and heads of state from all over. The interior of St. Matthew's Cathedral was filling up with mourners.

"Isn't that Richard Nixon?" Ralph asked.

"Yeah."

"Nice of him to show up. Kennedy mopped up the floor with him, in the debates."

They were silent for a while. Then Dickie spoke. "You know, this is kind of a nice place."

"You like it here?"

"I do. Think I'd be a good monk?" Dickie asked.

"You?" Ralph gave him a tap. "Are you serious? You?"

"Why not?"

"I'll tell you why not! No girls! Ever!"

"What do you mean? Don't they keep their wives and kids someplace else when they're chanting?"

"They have no wives, Dickie! No kids! They take a solemn vow. No wives, no girlfriends, not now, not for the rest of their lives, not ever! Just like your Uncle Holy Joe."

"You mean, never?"

"I mean never."

"How come?"

"They just do!"

"Yeah?"

"Yeah! For starts, you'd have to give up Dee Dee."

"Oh. Then I guess it's not such a good idea."

"Ridiculous, is what it is. You as a monk, go on with you!"

"Dad?"

"Yeah?"

"Me and Dee Dee broke up."

"Oh, yeah? Don't worry about it. Thousands of other girls will have you. Millions. You have your pick. And you get to do the picking; don't forget that."

They heard the monks continue to chant in Latin. Ralph never did do too well in that language. He could pick out the word *miserere.* Have mercy. And the names. S*ervus tuus Iohannes.* Your servant John. *Servus tuus Lyndon.*

Last night it had surprised him to hear the mercy chant include the name Lee Harvey Oswald. Father Albert explained: "He, too, is a child of God, even if he did commit this terrible sin. So, yes, we include him."

Ralph had to do some serious thinking about that. Asking for mercy for Oswald? It never would have occurred to him. Katie sure would not give him any.

Ralph and Dickie watched the rest of the funeral in silence. Ralph occasionally drummed his fingers. Dickie was remarkably still.

Ralph reflected: *Hozanner in Excelsis.* Latin. But darned if I can figure that one out.

Not till the end of the service did Ralph suddenly jump from his chair.

"Oh, no," he said softly.

"Oh, no, what, Dad?"

"Oh, Jeez."

The thought had occurred to him. Nashville, of all places?

That was a lot closer to Dallas, then it was to here.

And if the woman at the gas station were Katie. And if she had his gun.

"Dad?" asked Dickie.

Ralph bolted from the cell. He had to find Father Albert and plead with him. "Get your guys chanting again," he'd say. "Don't let it be Katie. And if it is, don't let her get near Dallas. Not with my gun. Please, God, don't let her!"

CHAPTER 29

The usual crowd showed up at Dan's house on Monday, but the mood was much more somber. Even Brunhilde curled up on the floor, subdued.

Claire had finally stopped weeping. She had heard the Naval Academy Choir singing the Navy hymn, *Eternal Father.* Her son Steven was among them. She would never forget. Who could?

Dan checked on the refreshments, but few were interested. He was sure that was Ralph and Dickie he saw on the park bench. How different from Claire's son, Dickie was. Steven Maldonato started out with two strikes against him. He was from a divorced household. His father was unreliable and unstable. Steven let nothing hold him back. He was going places.

Dickie had been handed every advantage and accepted them as his due. With all of that, he chose to go nowhere. A pity he never tried out for the T. S. Eliot football team, since he was a hollow boy growing up to be a hollow man.

"Let's hope Dickie can stay off camera for the rest of the day. Is that too much to ask?"

Dan took a quick look out the front window. There was still no one home at the Casey house.

"Look at that horse. He looks like a handful, but what a beauty. Wow." George observed.

"Ach," said Frieda. "Black Chack."

"He's got a mind of his own," Dan said.

Claire softly said, "He knows."

Then she started crying again. "Don't you see? He's like Whirlaway. He knows, and his heart is breaking."

Claire had to retreat to the kitchen. Even Dan broke down when he remembered Michelle and her one friend at St. Ethel's. A shot of Old Grand Dad helped them both. Only then could they return to see the rest of the service. Little more was said till the casket was lowered into the ground at Arlington.

"Oh, well, it's over now," said George. "Tomorrow, everything's supposed to be normal."

"Fat chance," Dan told him. "But there's one thing that had better happen."

"What's that?"

"Ralph and Dickie are going to be back."

"And Ralph is going to pay Joe what he owes. Every thin dime," Ma Casey observed.

"Let's hope," said Claire. "There's no way he's going to wiggle out of this one!"

"Add not the first time he's painted himself into a corner," Ma reminded them. "How well I remember it! There was Ralph, whining in the basement for someone to rescue him. How all my other boys laughed at him. Even Holy Joe. His father had a fit. Said he'd stay there till Hell froze over. Somehow, Ralph escaped. But did he learn his lesson? No."

Claire had decided to return to her own home, since there was no way Dickie could be waiting for her in the shrubs. Dan took her in the Porsche.

"Are you sure you feel up to being by yourself tonight?" he asked her.

"I'm sure. I needed that good cry. And thanks for the Old Grand Dad."

"'Twas nothing."

"And I don't want to impose on you and George anymore."

"Go on with you, you're no trouble."

"Can I ask you something, Dan?"

"Sure."

"You don't have to answer if you don't want to. Maybe it's none of my business. And maybe this is coming from Old Grand Dad, not from me. Do you love George?"

There was a long pause at a red light. "George and I are not related," Dan replied. "And George is from nowhere near Peoria. But yes, we love each other. Very much. And we want to spend the rest of our lives together."

"I thought so."

"We have to be so careful. How could you tell?"

"No one thing. Just the way you relate to each other."

"You realize that even today, in 1963, the world is not ready to accept this? George and I have to walk on eggshells. We hate the dishonesty. But the truth is I have no ex-wives, no kids, never did, never will. Suppose Ralph found out about us?"

Claire took a puff on her cigarette. "I don't want to think about that. One hundred megatons, for sure. That's why your secret is safe with me. But you're right. This is the modern era, we're so enlightened, but most people aren't ready to deal with this."

"Like my mother," Dan said as the light turned green. "She knows, but she can't handle it. Every time I see her, *it's when are you getting married, when do I get my first grandchild?*

Effie Mae has ten. I don't have any. If I won the Nobel Prize for Literature, it would be the same thing. That's why I don't see that much of her."

"Your mother sounds like Ralph." The light turned green. "Did you ever notice? There is Real World. And there is Ralph World."

"In Ralph World, Michelle fell into the bath tub and drowned. In Real World, there is a sealed death certificate that tells a different story. As does Michelle's diary, which he will never read."

"Because he's not ready to deal with it. And never will be. It doesn't fit into the narrow parameters of Ralph World."

There was another red light at Muratori Boulevard. "What do you suppose will happen, when Ralph World collides with Real World?"

"A disaster of Biblical proportions."

"Do you think they're on a collision course?"

"I do get that feeling." The light turned green.

"What about the feeling you had about Katie? That she's still alive?"

"I still feel it. She's alive out there somewhere, only I'm sensing that she's damaged in some way. As for where, I just don't know. She could be in Timbuctoo by now, for all we know."

The Porsche arrived at Claire's house. "Sure you'll be all right?" Dan asked.

"I am."

"I'll call you in the morning."

"Sooner, if anything happens? If Katie turns up?"

"Absolutely."

"Oh, Dan?"

"Yes?"

"I just wanted to say thanks. For getting me through this weekend from Hell. To you. And to George. I mean, you look at all the hate we've seen. And the misery it's caused. For Jackie, Caroline, John John, for the whole world. But you and George? You love each other. It's real. And it makes you strong. So, you could be strong for me. Your love should be honored, Dan. Not hidden, not ridiculed. Keep that in mind. Good night."

Dan watched until Claire was safely inside and her lamp went on. Then he put the Porsche in gear.

Your love should be honored.

Dan Doyle was beyond stunned. He never expected to hear such words in his lifetime.

CHAPTER 30

Ralph had no sleep on Monday night. Dickie was zonked out, but all Ralph could do was pace the corridors of the monastery. At midnight, he tossed on his coat and paced the pathways of the dormant garden for a few hours.

He'd gone to the abbot and explained that he was afraid Katie was in Dallas.

"Why do you believe that to be so? Did Katie ever express an intention to go to Dallas?"

"Well, no, but…."

"We cannot assume that, Ralph. We have no word of her whereabouts, not yet."

"But you don't know my wife. When she decides she's mad at you, oh boy, is she mad! Then she turns red and screams at you."

"Then, she settles down?"

"No, that's the thing. She stays mad. Goes from fire to freezer. She's not screaming and yelling any more, but she stays mad. Like with her sister Claire. I mean, Claire is the only sister she's got, no brothers. And she hates Claire. Froze her out. Won't have anything to do with her."

"A tragic situation, when a family splits apart like that," the abbot said. "Does Claire live in Dallas, is that it?"

"No. Claire lives close by. We just don't see her because Katie hates her so much. That's just an example of what happens when Katie's mad. Only when she loves somebody, it's just as crazy. And I think she loved Jack Kennedy. Thought about him all the time. I was sort of worried about it. Maybe she should have talked to a psychiatrist about it, I don't know. So that's why Dickie and I came to DC; we thought she was here for the funeral. But we didn't find her. And now I'm thinking…"

"You think she went to Dallas instead, to get revenge on Oswald?"

"Father Albert, I had a gun in the nightstand. It's gone, too. What am I supposed to think?"

"I see. Did you tell your brother she may be armed?"

"I did. He had to report that."

"You must know, some other misguided soul already murdered Lee Harvey Oswald."

"Yeah. I saw that on TV."

"Ralph, I know this is hard to accept, having your wife out there, missing, sick, probably armed."

"And she doesn't know how to use the damn thing, either. Excuse me, I shouldn't have said damn."

"Understood. But your brother Joseph has done the right thing and he is on top of the situation. He's got competent, professional people out there, looking for Katie."

"Yeah, but since I saw what happened to Oswald, I'd hardly call the Dallas police competent and professional."

"I can understand how you might feel about them. But again, we have no proof that is where Katie went. My best advice to you is to pray for Katie's safety and quick return."

Ralph sniffled.

"And get some rest tonight. In the morning, I'll take you and your son to the impound lot. You have a long trip home in front of you. Don't forget to call Joseph the minute you get there."

"I won't forget," Ralph promised. "I can't. My mother won't let me."

In the morning, Ralph did not feel well. He could not eat the breakfast he was offered. Dickie gladly put away both breakfasts.

"You must have a hollow leg," Ralph complained.

Then he was off to the impound lot. He paid as nastily as possible. Then he announced that there was a gouge on the driver's side door that was not there before. However, the gouge was documented as already being there, on the form filled out by the tow truck driver.

"Dammit to Hell!"

"Dad?" Dickie asked. "Can we just get back on the road? Please?"

"Yeah, yeah," Ralph said, and asked the lot attendant if he could use the men's room before leaving.

"That way. Bring this key back."

Ralph locked himself in the men's room. He regarded his image in the mirror over the sink. Terrible. And he felt as bad as he looked. He thought of the words of a popular commercial: "When your stomach is upset, don't delay!"

He turned around and projectile vomited, copiously, explosively, and triumphally, all over the tiny bathroom.

"That really hit the spot. I feel much better now. As they say on TV: fast, fast, fast relief."

He locked the door back up, returned the key without comment, got behind the wheel, and out of the District of Columbia by the fastest possible route.

Back at the monastery, Father Albert called Bishop Joseph to let him know that Ralph and Dickie were finally on their way back.

"Thank God for that," Bishop Joseph replied. "But I don't know if I can thank you enough for saving those two birds from themselves."

"Think nothing of it. Have you had any word about Katie yet?"

"Yes, less than an hour ago."

"Can you say where she is?"

"Dallas. Parkland Hospital, in fact."

"Oh, no! Ralph was concerned about that. How is she?"

"Not good, Albert. Several things going on here. She's had a massive stroke. Can't speak or move her right side."

"Lord have mercy on her."

"Plus, she'd not co-operating with the medical staff. Plus, she's had felony charges filed against her. She did commit a serious crime with a gun registered to Ralph."

"Did she kill anyone?"

"No. Apparently, she wandered into a high-end bar just as Oswald was shown being taken out of the police station."

"That's where Jack Ruby shot him."

"But no one in the bar saw that. Katie opened fire on the TV screen. Broken glass went flying. There were several serious injuries, including an oil man who lost an eye."

"Where do you stand now?"

"When Ralph gets back, he's going walk into a legal and medical nightmare. Right now, we have to get Katie extradited back to this state. But because of the serious nature of her crime, she's in a special unit for persons under arrest. There are police officers in her room, watching her. They tell me, even in her current condition, she did something awful. They had to shackle her to her bed."

"Can you say what she did?"

"She tore the sheet off Oswald's corpse and spat on it."

"What would possess anyone to do a thing like that?"

"I can honestly say, I don't want to know. But at least, any publicity about this incident will be at a minimum. There is simply too much other urgent news in the papers and on TV."

"But it's bad enough, Joe. Bad enough."

"Just pray that I'll be able to explain this to Ralph. He'll be home in a few hours. And at least in this family, Ralph is not famous for his stability."

CHAPTER 31

"I'm never going back there again! Never!" Ralph vowed. Then he thought for a while and said, "When you take your oath as a member of the United States Senate, then I'll go back. But not one minute sooner. And they'd better have a reserved parking space for me!"

"And a suite at the Mayflower?" Dickie asked.

"That, too."

They were well into Maryland. Traffic was still light. Ralph pulled to the side of the road.

"Something wrong?" Dickie asked.

Ralph got out of the car and dry heaved in the nearby woods. Then he came back and told Dickie he still didn't feel well. "Can you drive the rest of the way?"

"Sure," said Dickie.

"Here. You take the wheel. I'll just lie down in the back seat. But no funny stuff. Anyone wants to drag, ignore him. No getting pulled over, you hear me? You stay under the legal limit."

Dickie could not imagine who would want to challenge such a boring car to a drag race.

"I'll do it, Dad. If there's a hospital up ahead, you want to…"

"No! Just keep going. The only place I want to be is at home."

Ralph settled into the back seat and closed his eyes. He really was starting to feel pretty terrible. Maybe he ought to stop off at some emergency room. But, no. He could not afford to be sick now, therefore he wasn't.

He closed his eyes. Looking up at the endless barren trees made him feel more queasy. He closed his eyes and drifted into another place.

Many people were gathering around. This was some sort of demonstration. Up ahead he saw Avocet. She held up a placard. Ralph thought it said *We March for Jobs and Freedom. Up closer, it said I did not quit.*

He did not want to get into another dispute with Avocet, so he kept walking, deeper into the placard-carrying crowd. Yet few of the placards made sense. Dickie's said: I'm coming home in a box. What the Hell was that supposed to mean? Dan Doyle's said: Fear death by water. There was that half-brother of his with the message: *Consider John F. Kennedy, who was once as handsome and tall as you. Miss Emch: I should have stood up to the Board and told them NO MORE.*

"What the Hell is this?" Ralph demanded. "What place is this? What do all you people want? And why am I here?"

More people joined the crowd. Ralph saw Claire and thought, Katie had better not be here. If Katie sees her, she'll throw a fit.

Katie would have an even bigger fit if she saw what was on Claire's placard. *Ralph propositioned me several times. However, he'd had a few too many.*

Many others carrying placards joined the crowd. There were Ralph's co-workers, Ralph's family, Ralph's neighbors. Even the Wagners were there with Brunhilde on her leash. Brunhilde barked at him, and Frieda calmed her down in German.

At the base of a tree, Ralph heard pathetic whimpering. He saw wounded animal. It was curled up in a furry ball and its moans were becoming screams.

It must have been in terrible pain. "Can't anyone help this, whatever it is?" Ralph called to the crowd. No one seemed to hear him. Ralph was moved with pity for the poor thing.

Ralph's gun was in his pocket. He decided to put it out of its misery. He took aim, and then saw that it was not an animal at all.

It was a teenage girl in a full-length mink coat. The initials BVH were sewn into the lining.

Holy Joe took his gun and tossed it into a deep lake. "Do not do this," he said. "For she must do penance until the end of this world. Come with me, the orator is about to begin."

The crowd gathered around a speaker's podium. Who was that going to be? Martin Luther King? No, it was another young girl, with unbound hair, dressed in glowing white. She looked etherial, like the star of a silent movie. Her placard said: *I did not drown.*

"Joe," Ralph begged. "Let me out of here! I don't need to hear this. Let me go."

"You are not free to go yet," Joe replied.

The orator did not speak. Instead she put down her placard, rolled up her sleeves, and showed the crowd bright red scars on her wrists.

Ralph screamed.

CHAPTER 32

"Easy, Ralph," Joe sad. "It's OK. You're in Mercy Hospital."

"Back home?"

"You made it."

"But why?"

"It would appear that you picked up something nasty during your trip. That night on the park bench did not help. You were feverish and badly dehydrated. But now you are full of antibiotics and fluids and doing much better. That's what Dr. Robinson tells me."

"Who took me here? Dickie?"

"Dickie? Hah," said Ma Casey. "Didn't have enough sense."

"Well, he did get you home, at least. Then one of your neighbors saw that you were in such bad shape and called for help."

"Who? Who did that?" Ralph asked, hoping it was not that awful Dan Doyle.

"I honestly don't know," Joe admitted. "I wish I did know, so I could thank him or her. For all I know, it was the dachshund."

"She don't speak English," Ralph muttered.

"I should think not."

"No, she understands only German."

"I met Brunhilde. And I believe she understands a more universal language."

"You were there? At my place? And was Katie? Did she make it home, too?"

"We need to discuss this, Ralph."

"You found her?"

"Yes."

"Perhaps I'd better let you two talk about this," said Ma. The expression on her face was ominous.

"No, Ma, please stay," said Joe. "I want you in on this."

"If that's what you want."

"Where is Katie? Where did she go, what did she do?"

"Ralph, it's not good. She's very sick and in serious legal trouble."

"Why can't I see her?"

"Ralph, be calm. There are many problems here. In the first place, she's suffered a stroke."

"Really bad?"

"On her right side, and she can't speak. And it's not helping that she won't co-operate with the medical staff."

"Dr. Robinson said that might happen. If she didn't take her pills. You know, she left 'em behind. Dickie's got 'em. Where'd she go?"

"She went to Dallas."

"Dallas? Then I was right. Why hasn't she come back?"

"She's been arrested."

"Have them un-arrest her. She's sick, isn't she? You said…."

"Ralph, she committed a serious crime. With your gun."

"Didn't somebody else kill Oswald?"

"Yes, someone else did, though from what we can put together, that was her intention."

"To kill Oswald herself?"

"Yes. But you must understand this. When someone has a stroke, it's not always a fast thing. It can slowly occur, and apparently, that's what became of Katie. The stroke was in progress when she entered a bar in some high-class hotel."

"What was she doing there?"

"She was confused and disoriented. Several witnesses saw her quarreling with another woman outside the hotel. We don't know what the quarrel was about. And we do not know who this woman is. Then everyone started pouring into the bar, because there was a TV on, and Oswald was about to appear. Katie followed them in. When she saw Oswald, she opened fire on the TV screen."

"With my gun? The one I couldn't find?"

"It was registered in your name, yes."

"Anybody get killed?"

"No, but there were many severe injuries from broken glass. And more injuries, when a panic broke out and the exits were blocked. Therefore, she's been charged with a felony."

"No, no," said Ralph. "Not my Katie. She would not hurt a fly, you know that!"

"Ralph!" his mother warned him. "Please quiet down and listen to your brother. Katie's made a big mess and he'd trying his best to get her extradited from Texas, and…"

"No, no, no!" Ralph shouted. "I know Katie! We've been married for, how long? I forgot! But she'd never hurt anybody. Not even Lee Harvey Oswald, even if she had him in point-blank range. Don't you go telling me…"

The nurse came in, with a sedative. "I think we'd better go now, Ma," Joe said.

"You come back here!" Ralph ordered him. "You got no right to be saying those things about my Katie! Besides, that's not Katie in Dallas. It's somebody else. You didn't find her yet!"

"We'll be back," Joe promised him, "when you are more able to deal with this." He guided his mother to the elevator.

"I never did approve of that girl," Ma Casey said.

"Yes. Ma. I know."

"I knew she was trouble from the start."

"Yes, Ma."

"But is it possible that Ralph is right? The woman who shot up the bar in Dallas is someone else? You know what people are saying about the Dallas police, that they can't think their way out of a paper bag."

"I know, Ma. But they did this right. They looked in her wallet and found her driver's license. Katherine Q. Casey, 1409 Grimalkyn Lane. Also, the gun was registered to Ralph at the same address. I have to hand it to them. That was a job well done."

"Well," Ma said, exiting in the lobby, "She's gone and done it now. You didn't even get to the part of what Katie did to Oswald's dead body. Doesn't that bother you?"

"Yes, Ma. It does. More than I am letting on."

CHAPTER 33

"Mrs. Casey?" a nurse asked Katie.

"No, no, no!" Katie tried to say. *"My name is Katie Kennedy. I'm going to smack the next one of you who forgets that."* Only a growling sound came out.

"Your court-appointed attorney has been in touch with someone in your family. A Bishop Joseph Casey. He's trying to see about getting you extradited back home."

"Whatever that is, I don't need it. Call the White House, they'll tell you."

"Meanwhile, I've got your lunch."

"I am not going to eat that slop you call lunch." Katie tried to tip the tray over with her right hand. Nothing happened. When she tried with her left, it was caught in something. She could not pull it loose.

"Call the White House. Jack wants me to come back. Do it now, you fool. Before I get the Secret Service in here."

Katie turned away and kept her mouth and her good left eye closed. After a while, the nurse left. But the ghosts were coming back.

Time was spinning in reverse again, back to that terrible summer when Claire was so sick. Ma had vanished with her into the night, promising her father would return for her in the morning.

But he did not. He was far away, with Mrs. Keller. And Mother was not back the next day, either. Katie had left the house alone, even though she was forbidden to do so. Thus, she found herself in the field behind St. Patrick's when the ghosts arrived at dusk.

Again, she heard the roar of many engines and smelled the strong fumes of gasoline. How frightened she was to see ghosts, even though they could not see her behind the scoreboard.

Their eyes, she remembered. No eyes at all, but black holes leading to the emptiness of hollow skulls.

They spoke to one another, but Katie understood little of what they said. As they talked, they got to work, putting up three things. One was a judge's bench. Another was a large cross with no figure of Jesus on it, unlike the ones in St. Patrick's. Beside the cross was a gallows with a noose. A ghost called out, "All rise for the Grand Dragon!"

Another ghost, wearing many emblems, banged on the bench with his gavel. "This here honorable court is now in session! Bring forth the defendant!"

Two ghosts dragged a man up to the bench. He could not walk without help. But he was real. Not a ghost, but alive and real. Katie was certain of it.

"State your name!" the Grand Dragon demanded. The man said nothing. One of the ghosts slapped him and shouted, "You speak up when Hizzonner speaks to you, Boy!"

"He's too drunk to speak, Your Honor," said the other ghost. "His name is Al Smith."

"Al Smith!" the Grand Dragon thundered. "You stand charged with a whole bunch of crimes! You stand charged with a violation of the First Amendment of our Constitution! There shall be no amendment in regard to the (burp) establishment of any religion. And yet, you, Al Smith, you are attempting to get into the White House in order to impose the Roman Catholic religion on the rest of us!"

The other ghosts erupted into whoops and catcalls.

"That's right!"

"You, Al Smith, seek to make Roman Catholic marriages manda, manda, what's the word I'm looking for?"

"Mandatory, Your Honor," said one of the ghosts.

"Yeah! Meaning our own sons and daughters will be a bunch of little bastards. And what's worst of all, Al Smith, is that you have already set aside funds, millions of dollars of our hard-earned tax money…"

"Whoop! Whoop!" went the ghosts.

The gavel banged again. "Order in the court!" The ghosts quieted down.

"Millions of our dollars to construct a tunnel from the Vatican to the White House basement, under the Atlantic Ocean!"

The court erupted in to cheers.

"Millions, billions, in order to bring the very Tyrant of the Tiber, the pope himself, direct to our hallowed halls! To run this great nation right into the ground! To destroy our way of life! Order! I said, I want order in this here honorable court! Shaddap! That's better. Al Smith, how do you plead?"

The ghosts released Al Smith, who collapsed. Both ghosts kicked him.

"He pleads guilty, Your Honor," one of them said. "Guilty as all get out."

Katie watched the proceedings in growing horror from behind the score board. "Mommy!" she whimpered.

"All right, I've heard enough. Hang the drunken Irishman. Court's adjourned."

The gavel banged down. The Grand Dragon himself kicked Al Smith to the gallows, where two ghosts lifted him up and placed his neck in the noose.

There was a scream growing in Katie's throat, but it was trapped there. The bigger it got, the more it hurt. She felt the agony of the noose tightening around Al Smith's neck. But the ghosts were not done yet.

One of them tossed a lighted match at the cross. Soaked with gasoline, it broke into flames with a loud roar. The ghosts sang a song about an Old Rugged Cross. The flames spread to the gallows and consumed the still-living Al Smith as Katie watched with tears pouring down her face.

In the distance, sirens sounded. The ghosts quickly got back into their cars and drove away.

Katie curled up in a ball, frozen all over as was the scream, stuck in her throat.

<h1 style="text-align:center">CHAPTER 34</h1>

On a gloomy and dank winter day, three souls were gathered around a table in a downtown café. They were Dan, George and Claire.

"Ma Casey called," Claire told them. "Weren't we asking ourselves, what happens when worlds collide? When Real World crashes into Ralph World? Now, we know. Real World is a lot bigger. Ralph World gets smashed to smithereens. Here's how Ralph World ends: not with a bang but a whimper."

"Thank you again, T. S. Eliot," said Dan.

"Ma says that when he's not at work, all he does is sit around the house. Unshowered. Unshaven. In his robe and pajamas. All he does is watch TV and complain about it. Speaking of which, did you guys see Ed Sullivan last Sunday?"

"We did. That new British group. The Beatles," Dan told her.

"Yeah, yeah, yeah," George added.

"Here's what Ralph had to say about them: Caterwauling! No talent! I trust we've seen the last of them."

Dan snickered. "That's what he used to say about Michelle."

"I was thinking of her, too," said Claire. "If only she'd lived to see them, I bet she'd just love them. Which would only annoy Ralph even more."

"Ah, Ralph. It's true, I rarely see him out and about," Dan reported. "But the weather's been so lousy."

"It's more than that," said Claire. "He has not been to see Katie except for that one time. It convinced him, the poor soul really is Katie, who shot up a barroom in Dallas. Or what's left of her. Then he went home, turned on the TV, and started drinking. Ma's getting concerned about that."

Katie had been extradited from Texas and was now nearby, in the Tranquil Valley Nursing Home. Since Katie's arrival, it had been far less tranquil. The nursing notes from Parkland showed a lot of agitation. This tendency continued, along with a refusal to co-operate with speech, physical or occupational therapy.

"I was reading Michelle's diary last night," Claire told them. "And there was a quotation from a poem you recited to her once, Dan. Do you recall it? *The game is done! I've won! I've won! Quoth she, and whistles thrice.* What's that from?"

"The Ancient Mariner," Dan told her. "I can hardly imagine a worse omen. And yet, it says all, doesn't it? Death and Life-in-Death were playing dice on the deck of their ghost ship. Only this time, their ship went to Dallas. Death won Lee Harvey Oswald. Life-in-Death won Katie. But was a good thing you did, Claire, the way you brought her here."

Claire lit another cigarette. "Sometimes I wonder, why I even bother. What do I want? A round of applause? I'm not going to get it."

"What's this?" George asked.

"The extradition," said Dan. "Ralph's plan was to load Katie on a plane and ship her back. But Claire remembered, she'd never been on an airplane before. It was one of the things she was afraid of, so Claire made sure she was sedated for the trip. Ralph did not even think about that."

"That was decent of you," George said.

"Sometimes I think I'm too damn good, I don't know. But the bottom line is, this is such a mess and Ralph won't deal with it. Can the criminal charges be dropped, because of her condition? Is she able to stand trial? I very much doubt it. And even if the criminal charges are dropped, there still might be civil charges."

"Like the oil man who lost his eyeball?" George asked.

"He's only one example. But he has every right to sue, and he probably will. I sure would, were I in his shoes."

Claire gave her cigarette another puff. "Ralph's her legal next-of-kin. Ralph has power of attorney. Ralph won't get up off his arse and do anything. The only thing he's done right, is pay Holy Joe back for his big adventure. That's all, Folks!"

"I guess I never thought of it before," Dan said, "But Katie must have a lot of phobias, lurking inside her."

"Oh, that she does," said Claire. "Let's see. She was always afraid, afraid, afraid. Afraid of funerals and dead people. Afraid of, now this is odd! Afraid of Hallowe'en."

"How so? Don't most children love that?"

"When we were little and other kids came to trick-or-treat, she got scared and ran away. She had a problem with their wearing masks. If someone wore a ghost costume, she wanted no part of it. And she never went trick-or-treating herself."

"Weird," said Dan. "You'd think she'd want to load up on free candy."

"Yeah, you're right. Another thing she was afraid of: our mother's gas stove. I mean, she loves to eat, she just hates to cook over an open flame."

"George and I came up with something. Maybe Katie's biggest fear is of being abandoned. To your knowledge, Claire, was she ever abandoned?"

"I really don't think so!" Claire replied. "My parents had a lousy marriage, but I don't think they'd deliberately…oh, oh. Wait a minute!"

Claire had to pause a long time to dig up the memory.

"I had polio when I was four. Let's see, that must have been around 1928. Now, I don't remember that much about it. I just now remembered, I woke up in the middle of the night in a lot of pain, crying for my mother. And she was scared, because there was so much polio going around that summer. She needed to get me to the hospital right away. The trouble was, there was no one to stay with Katie, who must have been seven."

"Kind of young, to be left at home alone."

"Mother was desperate. She thought my father would be home in the morning."

"Now, he was the one with the mistress, right?" Dan asked.

"You said the secret word, you win one hundred dollars," Claire replied. "The communication between my parents was poor, since they could not stand each other. Now, Mom thought Dad was only spending the night with this Mrs. Keller. In fact, they had gone to Cape Cod, to make some whoopee.

"Katie woke up the following morning in an empty house. And the house stayed empty for most of the day. Mom was afraid I'd die if she left me at the hospital.

"Now, Mom being Mom, there was a good supply of food in the kitchen. But Katie was not used to being left alone. By around dinner time, Katie walked out of the house. Now she knew she was forbidden to do that. Or answer the door or the phone if no grownups were around. But she was getting frightened.

"I was too sick to understand what was going on. All of this, I heard much later. Mom got home after dark and Katie was gone. She was frantic and called the police."

"Then this is not the first time Katie has gone AWOL," George observed.

"Right. Then Dad got home and she tore into him. He insisted he'd gone out of town on business. "Monkey business!" she said. "One of your daughters is at death's door, the other is missing and this is how you act!" It's said she gave him a good boink on the head with her rolling pin, and was about to toss him out the door, when a police matron showed up at the door with Katie.

"Katie was in bad shape. She had been crying. Her dress was filthy. I never did find out where she had been or what she had done. But she was so upset, what came next was what the nuns call the Great Silence. She couldn't talk. She still could not talk when I got home. I don't recall how long that went on. I, being so terribly sick, was the center of attention. Maybe it was out of jealousy on her part. I never knew. I only knew that for a long time, Katie did not speak.

"Wow," said Dan. "She really was abandoned, then."

"And there's a big memory gap, too. Much later, I started asking questions. Do we know where Katie went? I came to think that she had been molested. A little girl, roaming the streets alone, so vulnerable. But Mom and Dad didn't want to talk about it. End of topic."

"Then there's quite a lot to Katie that no one knows," Dan said.

"As of now, it's all locked up inside her," Claire replied. "Unless someone can give her voice back to her. And she won't let me. That's why I have not been to the Tranquil Valley. No point in my getting her even more upset."

George had to get back to work. As they left, he asked Dan about Dickie.

"Which one?" Dan asked. "The mixed up white boy, or the white whale?"

"Either one. Surprise me."

"One of them is due to graduate from T.S. Eliot High in June, if he passes his exams. Big if there. And as for the other one…"

"Do tell."

"O.K. The gallant Charlie Ahab located the wreck of the Pequod at the bottom of the ocean."
"How?"

"Never mind how. It's complicated. Anyhow he got hold of the Spanish coin."
"Did it work, against the white whale?"

"Who knows? He managed to drop it. Plop! Back down to the bottom of the vast Pacific."
"Aw, no!"

"Aw, yes. See, the coin was like Dumbo's Magic Feather. It would have made no difference. What Charlie needs to do is find the ability within himself to defeat the white whale. Not in some external force."

"And did he?"

"He'd damn well better, before my editor loses patience with me. Anyhow the grand finale is coming up, a big explosion with tons of blubber filling the page. And the silver screen."

"I like it! Sign my copy, will you?"

"Consider it done."

CHAPTER 35

I don't like this place. I liked the other place better. They call it Parkland. I wish they'd send me back there. Jack was there for a while but he's all right now, thank God.

I don't even know how I got here. I suspect someone is giving me drugs, trying to poison me. They think I don't know this, but I do. Someone is jealous. The Secret Service has been put on notice.

I'll tell you who came to see me. Ralph Casey. I can't imagine who let him in. I tried to tell him to go away but the words still won't come out. I think he got the message, though, since he never came back. Maybe he's not as stupid as he looks.

Not that I care. I have plenty of other responsibilities to worry about. Tonight, for instance, is a state dinner for the president and first lady of, oh, I can't recall the name of the place. It's one of these emerging African nations with a name a mile long. Which gown should I wear? Jack likes seeing me in the pale blue one. Or do you prefer the green?

My name is Katie Kennedy. I'd like to welcome you to the White House. Who might you be?

The day nurse wrote that Katie seemed calmer. Last night there had been some major agitation. A stronger sedative was needed.

Last night, even more came back.

Katie was curled up in a ball, in terror, behind the score board. Once the ghosts had fled, the fire department took over. Then the police came.

One had a flash light to look behind the score board. "Hey! Over here!" he called to the others. He had to bend down to reach Katie.

"And what's this?" he asked in a thick Irish brogue. "A little girl? Such a pretty one, too. What might your name be?"

Katie could not say.

"Well, now. I'm not a gambling man. But if I were, I might bet that your name is Katherine Marie Quinn, am I right?"

Even though Katie knew she must not speak to strangers, Mother said it was all right to talk the police. In fact, it was encouraged, if one got lost. Still she could not reply.

"Oh, my Lord!" said the matron, crawling on her hands and knees to reach Katie. "Honey, did you see what they did? Did it scare you?"

"Did it?" the other officer asked.

"She can't talk," said the matron. "She must have seen." To Katie she said, "Sweetie, do you know what an effigy is? Hmmmm?"

No reply.

"An effigy is like a dummy. You know, like in the shows at then Bijou? They pretend to talk, but it's someone else's voice? It's not a real live person. It's something stuffed with straw and dressed up. To look like a real person. Like a scarecrow in a suit. You understand? That's what the bad men burned. Not somebody real. Honey, can you hear me?

It was a real live person. I saw him! His name is Al Smith and they hanged him and burned him alive! Katie tried to say.

"We have to get her back home," said the matron, picking up the squirming Katie. "Mrs. Quinn is worried sick. And she has another wee one with polio, in the hospital."

"Jaysus," the Irish cop said. "Too much for any one mother."

Katie remembered being back in her room, in her own bed. Her parents were talking to the police downstairs. She heard her mother's gasp of horror.

"Are you telling me it was the Ku Klux Klan, did this?"

"That it was. No question," the Irish policeman replied. "There were plenty of witnesses."

"But I thought they were only in the Deep South!"

"No, Ma'am, they're here. They're everywhere. It's this campaign, bringing them out of the holes in the ground they live in. Herbert Hoover versus Al Smith. They can't stand the idea of Smith, being a Catholic, getting into the White House. So, they held a kangaroo court, found Al Smith guilty, and hanged him in effigy. Then they burned a cross, along with the effigy."

"Right in St. Patrick's field!" her father exclaimed. "Is no place safe anymore?"

"The effigy was full of dry straw, went right up."

"And Katie had to see that," said her mother. "My poor babies! How can we raise Catholic children in an atmosphere so poisonous? Can nothing be done?"

"What you must understand is this. The Klan keeps itself invisible. That's why they don't show their faces when they're out doing the harm they do. They take their sheets off their beds and wear them. And they put their pillowcases over their heads. You don't know who they are.

You might sit down beside someone on the bus and not know he's been running around in his sheets all night, burning crosses and acting like a savage."

"Oh, dear. Oh, dear."

"Now, if 'twere up to me, I'd take the whole lot of them, tar and feather them, and run them out of town on a rail. But it's not. Sniveling cowards, all of them, afraid to show their ugly faces. Can't call themselves men. My advice to you would be, keep a close watch on both your girls. At least till this miserable campaign is over."

After the police left, Katie heard her mother sobbing softly.

'Now, Dear, Katie's home safe and everything's going to be all right," her father said.

"No thanks to you! When are you going back to your little snookie-poo?"

"Rose was very worried about both the girls."

"I'm sure she was!"

The next day, her father was still there. He was reading his paper and showed her a picture. "See? Here is the real Al Smith. And here is where he really was yesterday, making a speech in Boston. Nobody did anything bad to him."

Katie turned away. *I know what I saw, she thought.*

"Please!" her mother warned him. "Katie is never going to get over this if you keep reminding her. It's best that we don't talk about this. Ever again."

1978

CHAPTER 36

Katie lived for another fourteen years. She was buried at Holy Cross Cemetery under a marker that read:

Husband

Ralph Waldo Casey

1918-1969

Wife

Katherine Marie Casey

1921-1978

Together Forever

Not far away was a park bench with a plaque:

In Loving Memory

Michelle Elaine "Mimi" Casey

1946-1962

At least Dickie's marker did not say Dickie. It said:

Richard Quinn Casey

1944-1968

Viet Nam

Dickie was not in Holy Cross. He ended up in Arlington, close to John F. Kennedy.

Though no one cared to admit it, Ralph died of alcoholic cirrhosis of the liver. He was the first, although the youngest, of the Casey brothers to die. Katie died of the long-term effects of her stroke.

Ralph never got over the destruction of Ralph world. Therefore, he drank. Even after his legal team got the criminal charges against Katie dropped, based on her impairment, he was still bitter and unhappy.

He turned to Holy Joe and said, "When do I get my gun back?"

"For the love of God, Ralph, it was used as evidence. There is no way the Dallas police, or any police department, is going to give it back to you. They melt those things down."

"I still want it back."

Katie never really regained her words. There came a time when Claire could visit. As a peace offering, she gave Katie what was left of their disputed Baby Jane doll. "Do you remember?" Claire asked. "Mother said to give it back to you."

In response, Katie snatched the doll's head away with her good hand and rocked it like a real baby, repeating *mi, mi, mi, mi.*

"Mimi," said Ma Casey. "Like in the opera, La Boheme. That's what I called Michelle when she was a baby."

"Good Lord, what have I done?" Claire asked Ma.

"Your best. That's all any of us can do."

No one could take the head away from Katie. Not even when Katie made a mess, trying to feed her meals to Baby Jane.

Katie never let anyone else touch her doll's head, but after a while she calmed down to the point where Claire no longer upset her. She talked to Claire, but only in a stream of sounds that made sense only to Katie.

Do I know who you are, Dear? You look so familiar, I just can't recall who you might be. Anyhow, things have gone so well. Jack defeated Barry Goldwater by a landslide in 1964. His second Inauguration was splendid. We were married by Cardinal Cushing at St. Matthew's the night before. Oh, the whole family has been so kind and accepting of me, including his mother Rose. Sadly, his father Joe had that stroke and cannot speak, but seems to be glad to see me. Bobby and Teddy are so much fun. I suppose I will have to get used to these touch football games.

Did you see Jack and I dancing at the Inaugural Ball? I wore my wedding gown, which is now in the Smithsonian. With the other First Ladies' gowns. Go see it when you're in Washington. And there's more. Now, the press release is not out yet, so don't breathe a word of this to a soul! Promise? But there will soon be the pitter-patter of little feet in the White House again. Yes, I'm going to have a baby! December, the doctor says. Remember, mum's the word!

"Apparently, she's forgotten who I am," Claire reported. "She's only able to produce a word salad. I'm sure it's a scathing denunciation of me, not realizing I'm taking in the whole thing."

Rarely Katie spoke in real words, forgot what she was saying, and gave up. "Where is he?" she asked Claire. "He was just here. Where did he go?"

"Who, Katie? Who is he?"

"Hunh."

Another time Katie woke up suddenly and stated, "In the middle!"

"The middle of what?" Claire asked.

Katie gave her a look that said, *are ye daft, Girl? You asked the question, I answered it. In the middle!*

Mostly she spoke in nonsense syllables. Claire told Dan that some of the sounds repeated at regular intervals.

"It's like the refrain of an epic poem."

"Could well be," Dan agreed. "When I had to do all that research on whales, I heard some recordings of the songs of humpbacks. And some of them have that same thing, a repeating refrain. We can't translate their language. Yet. But I came to think, it was an epic poem, about a battle with an insane one-legged human. Their side of the story."

Moby Dick II: Raise the Pequod spent several weeks on top of the New York Times best seller list. The film was a blockbuster but soundly panned by the critics. It only won one Oscar, for special effects. The love theme from the inane romantic subplot (which was not in the book) made the Top Ten and is still heard on elevators everywhere.

Ma Casey was still alive, sharp as a tack, and rapidly approaching a three-digit birthday. She and Claire would always be friends, though Claire did envy her for having one long happy marriage, so unlike her own or that of her parents.

"What was our secret?" Ma asked. "Rarely did we fight! After any given day, dealing with eight boys, we were too darn tired!"

Claire had to laugh. The thing about Ma was, although she could be wickedly snide, she was funny. And so was the man she married. Unlike her own parents, they were crazy about each other. Oh, were they ever! Eight kids? It showed!

The remaining Casey brothers were all doing well. Jimmy had expanded Casey Chevrolet to three different locations. But Ma's pride and joy was still her first, the one they called Holy Joe, now Joseph Cardinal Casey.

On an early Fall morning, Ma and Claire were part of the entourage taking Cardinal Casey to the airport for his flight to Rome. As he reminded them, for the second election of a new pope in the same year.

"Made up your mind, who you're going to vote for?"

"Shucks, Ma, I can't tell you that!"

"Seriously," Claire asked, "has this happened before?"

"I'll have to look that up. It may have, way back when Nero was feeding us to the lions."

Ma and Claire watched on the observation deck till Joe's flight vanished into the sky. It was going to JFK, of all places, for a connecting flight to Rome. Then Claire drove Ma home, but not directly.

"We'll take the scenic route," Ma decided. "Down Muratori Boulevard. Memory Lane. I'll show you some things."

Claire pulled out of the parking lot. "You know something?" Ma asked. "I very much doubt they'll elect an American."

"But, Ma, if they did? If Joe won?"

"It would go right to my head. There would be no living with me. What a pain in the rear I'd be! Besides, I'm too old to have to deal with a bunch of reporters. And what do they call those crazy camera boys running around Rome?"

"Paparazzi, Ma."

"Paparazzi, is it? Just as well. Have you heard from Dan? Since he…oh, what was that word?"

"Out, Ma. He came out and published the truth about himself. He's gay, and proud of it. If anyone has a problem with it, it's their problem, not his."

"Ah."

"His books are still selling like hotcakes. He did get some negative feedback. I saw some of the hate mail he got. It made my skin crawl. But Dan doesn't throw that stuff away. He puts it in his idea file. That way, he can throw it back at where it came from."

"I always did admire his spirit. Oh, turn here."

Once on Muratori, Ma pointed out an office tower. "That's where our home was. That's where I raised all my boys. We had a grand Victorian, right there, with a wraparound front porch. And a tree in the front yard, with a tire swing. And a lawn that was stomped into nothing."

"One might expect that, with eight boys."

"At least they had another place to go and let off steam. That's St. Patrick's church, up ahead. They had quite an athletic program back in those days. Baseball, football, you name it, they had it. Kept a lot of boys out of trouble, including my own."

"That's great, but how was it possible? The church buildings take up most of the block."

"You see that McDonald's?"

"Yes. Did you want to go in?"

"No, thank you. It's one of my secrets of a long life. Avoiding what they call food. Anyhow, where the McDonald's is, plus the parking lot, all of that was St. Patrick's field."

"Was it, now?"

"That's where they had the fire."

"There was a fire? At St. Patrick's? I never heard of it!"

"And that's the pity of it. People forget."

"When did this happen?"

"In 1928."

"I remember that year so well, because that's when I had polio. But I never heard anything about a fire."

"No one wanted to talk about it."

"Why not? Fires always get a lot of talk. Isn't that right?"

"This was in 1928. Terrible things were going on. People were afraid."

"Was it arson, was that it?"

Ma kept gazing at the McDonald's.

"It was an election year," Ma said. "Perhaps you were too young, or to sick, to know that. And a more vile excuse for an election, you never saw. Herbert Hoover. And Al Smith."

Claire smacked her forehead. "Yes!" she said. "Al Smith was the first Catholic to run, and that's why he lost!"

"But there was more," said Ma. "Much more. There were rumors, lies going around, that no rational person could believe. Still, many believed them. That if elected, Al Smith would get rid of any boundary between his church and the state. He'd have the pope running our government. To that end, he would have a tunnel built between the White House and the Vatican."

"Heckuva long tunnel!"

"People believed this nonsense, Claire, even around here. We were viewed with contempt and suspicion. And then one night, the Ku Klux Klan made its presence known."

"That could not be possible, not here."

"More than possible. They burned a cross in St. Patrick's field, along with an effigy of Al Smith."

Claire was too stunned to say anything.

"I remember it well, I'd just gotten the boys washed up, prayers said, and was tucking them in their beds. Rather like a Norman Rockwell painting, don't you think? Freedom from fear. But it was Ralph who told me, 'Ma, I smell smoke.' And I looked out his window and sure enough, I saw column of flame rising from what I thought was the church. I called the fire department. Then ran out to the front porch. The fire engines went tearing up Muratori, and what went the other way, was a line of cars filled with men in bed sheets. One of them shook his fist at me. Shouted I'd better vote for Hoover, or they'd be back. Freedom from fear? I've never been so frightened in my whole life."

"Aw, Ma! All this time and I had no idea!"

"When you don't talk about these things, people forget. They build a McDonald's over it, pave it over, and pretend it never happened."

"Al Smith lost the election, and what did we get instead? The world's worst economist. What did that radio announcer call him? Hoobert Heever."

"The Great Depression. Years of misery."

"Ma, I knew that some bad things went on during the Kennedy campaign. He had to explain himself, that he would not be taking orders from Rome. But still, nothing that bad, not that I knew of, at least. Aw, Ma, I'm so sorry you had to live through that."

"Don't be, Dearie," Ma said, touching Claire's arm. "It wasn't pleasant. It wasn't easy, getting through that campaign, and such a humiliating defeat at the end. But I have to say this. It's part of what made me the person I am today. Were my life a bed of roses, I'd be different. Most likely, a sticky little Pollyanna who would bore the socks off you."

"You, boring, Ma? You're anything but!"

"Well, then. You see my point."

Claire drove up to Ma's front door. "Yes, I've had my share of hardship. One thing I can say. When I look back at that '28 campaign, I hope that I never, and I mean never, see anything that ugly again. If I do, I ask only for the strength to get through it. And I hope, Claire, I hope you never have to see it either."

"I'd rather think we're beyond that."

"I'd like to think that, too," Ma said as she got out of the car.

"Can you make it in?" Claire asked her.

"Sure, what do you think I am? Old?"

"Ma, you are a card!"

"Oh, one thing. Say hi to Dan and George for me, will you?"

"I'll do it, Ma. I'll do it," Claire promised, and merged back into the traffic on Muratori.

Remember what happened here, she told herself. They tell us to ask not. They replace, they bury, they gloss over, they remain silent.

But there is so much under the ground. You cannot be complete without knowing what is truly there.

So, ask.

***

The Banana Boat Song, 1957, RCA Records, traditional Jamaican folk song

Death by Water sequence from *The Wasteland,* T. S. Eliot, 1922

Game is Done sequence from *The Rime of the Ancient Mariner,* Samuel Taylor Coleridge, 1834

Editorial Assistance by Butler Design Services, Hyattsville MD

Many thanks to Linda Strader and Maggie Berry for invaluable feedback.